I reached for the flask a...
belt, unscrewed the ca...
coursed its way down ...
could feel my blood be...
veins. I took another m...
until it was empty, and I raised my lips to his.

He unbuckled his belt, took the flask from my hand,
threw them both behind him, and his mouth came
down to meet mine. It was his turn to drink from my
lips, and we kissed for a second time, our mouths
pressed hard together, our tongues duelling, our teeth
clashing.

My hands slipped down his back, inside the wetsuit,
until I was holding his buttocks . . .

HONEY

A girl's tantalizing sexual education

Also available

BLONDE
BRUNETTE
REDHEAD
SCARLET

ANGELIQUE

WARNER BOOKS

A Warner Book

First published in Great Britain in 1992
by Warner Books

Copyright © Suzanne de Nîmes 1992

The moral right of the author has been asserted.

A CIP catalogue record for this book is available
from the British Library.

ISBN 0 7088 5376 5

Phototypeset by Intype, London
Printed and bound in Great Britain by
BPCC Hazells Ltd
Member of BPCC Ltd

Warner Books
A Division of
Little, Brown and Company (UK) Limited
165 Great Dover Street
London SE1 4YA

Chapter One

I was wearing a pair of sunglasses, expensive designer-brand mirror-shades.

I walked along the edge of the beach, the warm waves washing over my feet. The sea was turquoise, the sand was white. High above, the sun blazed down from the cloudless sky.

'Don't smile,' Rick told me.

'I can't help it, I'm happy.'

'Don't smile,' repeated Rick, whom I'd never seen smile.

It was hard to look at him without smiling. It was obvious that he didn't like the sand, because he was wearing a pair of plastic sandals; and he kept well away from the water because he didn't like to get his feet wet. Although wearing a pair of shorts, Rick still had his white business shirt on – but at least he'd removed his tie. A place like this was wasted on him. He was wearing a straw hat to mask the sun, and his face was hidden by his camera. He stared at me through the viewfinder, and the motordrive went into action as he took several rapid shots.

This was the reason we were here, why we had travelled thousands of miles – so that Rick could take a series of photographs of me.

As I said, I was wearing a pair of sunglasses.

Just a pair of sunglasses . . .

And it was a series of nude photographs.

We could have done all this on the beach of my home town, I thought. But it wouldn't have been the same. The rocks and the stones, the seaweed and all the washed-up rubbish would have spoiled the image;

and we'd have had to spend hours waiting for the rain to stop and the sun to come out.

That wasn't the way I remembered it, but it was the way that the place had appeared when I last went home. It had become smaller, dirtier, run down and decayed.

As a kid, however, it had been a great place to grow up. What I remembered most were the long summers of childhood, when it seemed that the sun was always shining, and when we'd never heard of the word 'pollution'. These days, I'd never have dared venture into that dark and cold sea; but we never noticed the cold. It had been our desert island, as wonderful to us then as this tropical beach was to me now . . .

'Shall we go for a swim?'

'What – now?'

'Yeah, now.'

Helen and I had been out for the evening, ended up at a club, and were now walking home along the seafront. It was a calm night, and we both felt warm from all the dancing we'd done. The sky was black, speckled with stars; the moon was half-full, low upon the horizon. The tide was perfect for swimming, the gentle waves lapping over the sand.

We had often gone for midnight dips together; and we'd already had several moonlit swims this summer, even though it was early in the season.

'But we haven't got any costumes,' I said.

'So what? There's no one around. Who's there to see us?'

'Well . . . you'll see me.'

'That's the only drawback, I suppose.'

She ducked as I playfully swung my bag at her.

'Anyway,' she added, 'you haven't got anything I haven't got. Have you?'

'I hope not.'

We halted and leaned against the rail on the promenade. The idea of a swim was very tempting, but I wasn't too enthusiastic about going in naked. I gazed over at the sea. Because it was so dark, I couldn't see if anyone else was on the beach. But that would mean no one could see us, I realized, and the water would be so refreshing. I glanced at Helen, wondering if she was bluffing.

'Okay,' I said.

'You mean it?'

'Yes.'

'The pier?' asked Helen, doubtfully.

At night, we usually went in by the pier. It was a useful landmark, because we could easily find where we'd left our clothes. We weren't the only ones who went swimming from there, however – and, no matter how dark, I didn't want to go skinny-dipping if there were other people around.

I looked over to the pier, which was about half a mile away. It was hung with lights, far too public.

'Here,' I said, and I started down the concrete steps which led to the beach. I wouldn't go in alone, and I wondered if Helen would follow. She did. We took off our shoes and walked across the stones and pebbles and shells. We had both lived here all our lives; our feet were tough. When we reached the sea, we walked straight in and the waves washed over our feet and lapped around our legs. We waded in knee-deep, hitching up our skirts.

It was as if we had reached the edge of another world. I glanced back to where the seafront buildings were lit by the glowing streetlamps and the intermittent flashes of car headlights. The wall beneath the promenade was like the ramparts of a castle, built to hold back the invading oceans. It might succeed for a century or two, but in time the town would inevitably be invaded by the remorseless waves. Engulfed by the tide, it would all be swept away – exactly as had happened to the ancient village which had once

7

existed a mile from where Helen and I now stood. The lost village lay forever drowned, claimed by the sea.

It was the sea from which humanity had come, evolving from creatures which had crawled ashore countless millions of years ago. And for some of us, the lure of the ocean was still very strong . . .

We glanced at each other and nodded, then headed back up the beach. The sand was wet beneath our feet, indicating that the tide was going out. We halted a dozen yards away, by one of the breakwaters, and I put my shoes and bag down on the huge timber support.

'Will our things be okay?' asked Helen.

'Who'd want them?' I had no valuables in my bag, hardly any money left.

'We haven't got any towels.'

It had been Helen's idea to go swimming, but she had become the reluctant one. By now, I was determined to go into the water.

'You stay and look after my stuff,' I told her. 'And afterwards I'll run up and down to get dry.'

Helen laughed, then glanced all around. There was no sign of anyone on the beach. The only movement was of the waves across the sand, the only sound that of the water. Helen watched as I unfastened my blouse, and then she removed her own top. We shed our skirts simultaneously. Clad only in our underwear, we looked at each other.

I was sure that Helen had meant that we should go swimming in the nude, but maybe I had misunderstood. Perhaps our undies would suffice as costumes.

Then Helen reached behind and unfastened her bra, and I gazed at her suddenly exposed breasts. The night wasn't as dark as it seemed: her boobs were in clear view, and her nipples were hard.

All I could do was repeat her action, and I shed my bra. We looked at each other's moonlit tits.

8

'I didn't realize you were such a big girl,' Helen remarked.

'Ha! Look who's talking!'

We both smiled. We were best friends, but it was years since we'd been young enough to venture into the sea wearing only our knickers. We'd both grown a lot since then, and since then we'd stripped down to our underwear together many times, spending frequent Saturday afternoons in clothes shops, trying on different outfits and wishing we could afford them.

In many ways, Helen and I were exact opposites. She was the extrovert. I'd never have suggested a nude midnight swim; but if someone showed the way, I'd be willing to follow. I was always the shy one at school, trying to hide at the back, never volunteering an answer even when I knew it. Helen was a good person for me to go around with, because she was never reticent, was always willing to try something new and daring.

When we were younger, Helen had been taller and fatter than me, but by now she had slimmed down – while I had grown up. We were about the same height, the same dimensions, which was why we could wear each other's clothes. Helen's hair was very curly, which I envied, and jet-black. Mine was corn-gold, but every summer the sun and the sea ripened it to wheat-blonde. We both wore our hair very short, because then it would dry quicker after we had been in the water.

Helen's hair had grown longer since last year, however, and short hair didn't seem such a good idea any more. It might be functional, but it wasn't so attractive. These days, I hated the way that the briny water left my hair so unmanageable, and I always rinsed the salt away after I'd been swimming. But at least tonight no one would see what the water did to my make-up.

I hooked my thumbs into the elastic of my briefs. Helen did the same with her panties. We looked at one another, then stripped off together and stood totally naked in front of each other. We would never have done so in the daytime, but I was surprised how much of her I could see in the moonlight. The black triangle of Helen's pubic hair was fully visible against her pale flesh. In contrast, my own fair curls seemed to blend in with my skin.

I was standing naked on the beach, I realized. Totally nude. It was the first time I had ever stripped off in the open – and it felt completely natural.

Helen suddenly yelled: 'Last one in is . . . !'

Already she had started running down the beach, and I chased after her.

We hit the water together, plunging into the waves and diving beneath the surface.

And it was great.

Without clothes, I was more a part of the ocean than ever before. Eighty per cent of the world's surface is water; eighty per cent of the human body is water. We are far more aquatic than we believe. I immersed myself completely, becoming as one with the ocean. When I came up for air, I saw the moon, and I was also a part of that. Its primordial rhythms pulsed through my veins.

I'd always worn a one-piece costume for swimming. I'd tried bikinis, but they were never very practical; they were designed to be seen in, not for swimming. I seemed to spend most of the time trying to make sure that the bra didn't slip off or the pants fall around my knees, dragged down by the waves.

Swimming in the nude was the ideal solution. I'd never felt so free before. I lay on my back, gazing down at myself, at my nipples which protruded above the surface, at my pubic hairs which rippled in the water like some exotic ocean plant. It seemed such a stupid idea to put on clothes to go into the sea, but I supposed that there was no alternative. I didn't want people looking at me. Not strangers, anyway. But it didn't matter with Helen.

Was it different because she was a girl? I didn't think so. Female or male, I didn't want to be seen naked by anyone.

Helen and I swam up and down for quite a time. All the while I was watching that we didn't drift too far away from the beach where we'd left our clothes; and she must have been doing the same.

'Let's get back,' said Helen finally, as she swam up to me.

'Okay,' I said.

She stood up, water dripping from her body. The sea level was at her waist. As the waves retreated, they exposed her dark pubic hairs. She looked wonderful in the pale light, moonbeams reflecting from the drops of water which speckled her nude flesh. I tried not to look, but there was nowhere else to focus my eyes. So I also stood up, and Helen was as interested in me as I was in her.

'That was great,' I said, tossing my hair back to shake the water free.

Such an action also had the effect of making my breasts bounce up and down; and I noticed that Helen was looking at the motion of my boobs. She realized that I was watching her watching me, and she smiled.

'Yeah, it was,' she agreed, and she shook her own head, and her breasts swayed.

For the first time I realized why guys were so fascinated by girls' breasts. I knew all about my own, but Helen's naked tits looked so intriguing, firm yet soft. I found myself wondering how they would feel if I touched them, and I instantly banished the thought from my mind.

We waded ashore, water dripping from our naked torsos and down our bare limbs. The ocean had seemed cold at first, but I had soon become used to it. Now I felt colder away from the sea and wanted to

11

get dressed quickly. I was covered in goose pimples, and my nipples were fully erect. We hurried up the beach to where our things were – but they weren't there . . .

'Is this the wrong beach?' asked Helen, as she glanced around.

I noticed our earlier footprints in the sand, and I said: 'No.'

'Where are our clothes? I'm getting cold.'

'Come over here,' said a male voice, 'we'll warm you up.'

Two shadows appeared on the other side of the breakwater. I immediately covered myself as best as I could, one hand over my crotch, the other over my breasts. Helen didn't bother, either because it was too late or because she didn't care. She put her hands on her hips and turned towards the two guys who were watching us.

'Danny?' she said.

'Er . . . no,' said the voice, which I now recognized as Danny's. He was in our class at school.

'And is that Simon?' asked Helen.

'Hello, Helen,' answered Simon, who was also in our class. Like Helen and I, Danny and Simon were always together.

'What are you doing down here?' Helen asked.

'We've been swimming,' replied Simon. 'Like you.'

'Have you got our clothes?'

'No,' said Danny.

'Yes,' said Simon. 'No.'

'No,' said Danny. 'Yes.'

'No,' said Simon.

'No,' said Danny.

It was obvious that they had taken our stuff, but only as a joke – why else would they want it? If there had been any other reason, they would already have disappeared with it. They must have been swimming before us, but we hadn't seen them because they were on the other side of the breakwater. When they heard us coming, they had kept quiet, which probably meant they had been watching while we undressed.

'Are you going to give us our clothes back?' asked Helen.

'No.'

'Yes.'

'Yes.'

'No.'

'Come on,' Helen said to me. 'Let's go home.' She started walking up the beach.

I didn't move. Helen couldn't have been serious, could she? We both lived about half a mile inland. Was she really intending to walk home naked? Across the main seafront road, then up the side streets until she reached her house? It was late, it was quiet – so maybe she did. But I wouldn't have dared to.

I watched her go, and then I glanced at Danny and Simon. Their heads were turned; they were also staring at her.

'Wait, Helen, wait!' called Danny.

She halted, but didn't turn. 'What?'

'You can have your clothes if . . . '

'If what? If we show you our tits?' asked Helen, and I couldn't help laughing.

Show us your tits! Show us your tits! That was the favourite chant of the boys at school. It had started when they yelled at the girls playing sports, as they gazed at our boobs bouncing up and down while we ran; but before long they shouted it at every opportunity. When they could be sure of being unidentified, they would even call out to the younger female teachers: *Show us your tits!*

Some of us had come up with a retort: *Show us your pricks! Show us your pricks!* But we'd decided against using it, partly because we didn't want to encourage them and partly because they probably would have obeyed. The male of the species needed little excuse to drop their pants, or so I'd heard – and I later discovered that was absolutely true.

I could hear whispers as Danny and Simon debated what to do next. While they were distracted, I wondered if I could leap over the breakwater and grab my clothes. But I didn't really want to get any closer to them. Being nude, I felt at a distinct disadvantage.

'If you give us a kiss,' came the answer.

That was no big deal. I'd been swimming with both Danny and Simon, they were regulars amongst the under-the-pier gang. We'd known each other for years, although it was only recently that the female members of our group had paid much attention to the male. And vice-versa. No longer kids, we were almost grown – in some respects we *were* grown – and we were naturally interested in the opposite sex.

I'd already kissed Danny. I'd already kissed Simon. They'd both had their tongues inside my mouth, but neither of them was very good at it. In order to retrieve my clothes, I was prepared to suffer again.

'Okay,' I said. I was still doing my best to protect my modesty, even though they must have seen me strip off and had already watched me walking naked up the beach.

But how much had they seen? Helen had gone only a few yards away and was almost lost to sight. Although they were on the other side of the breakwater, I could hardly see Danny or Simon. If it hadn't been for their voices, I wouldn't have recognized them.

'Not okay,' said Helen, but she turned and came back. 'What are you wearing?'

'Our swimsuits,' Danny answered.

'Take them off.'

'Helen!' I hissed.

'I know what I'm doing,' Helen whispered as she reached my side.

I doubted that she knew what she was doing. We

14

seemed in no position to negotiate conditions. There was no reason why the boys should agree.

Helen stood brazenly naked, and I felt kind of stupid with my hands across myself. What did it matter if Danny and Simon saw me? Nothing, I realized, and I let my arms fall. We gazed at the two shadowed shapes ahead of us.

'Then what?' asked Danny.

'Come over here and find out. You might get more than a kiss.'

'Helen!' I repeated.

She stood with her hands on hips, legs astride, and she was grinning.

'Or if you're too scared,' Helen added, 'just throw us our clothes and we'll go home. Maybe you haven't got the balls for it . . . '

This time I was too amazed to say anything.

'You've got our clothes,' she added, 'so give us yours. Throw us your swimsuits, then come over here.'

Originally, only their heads had been silhouetted over the breakwater; by now, the top halves of their bodies were in view. They were whispering to each other. One of them wanted to do as Helen asked, the other didn't. There was a cloud over the moon, and I couldn't see which was which, but I could guess that it was Danny who was in favour of the idea. He was the pushy one of the two.

'Okay,' said Danny and he threw something onto the ground between us. It was his swimsuit. He climbed over the breakwater and jumped onto the sand.

'Let's see if you're all talk,' he said.

My heart was beating faster now. I'd never been so close to a naked boy, and I couldn't really see that much in the darkness – but I turned my head, not wanting him to know I was looking at him. Taking that as his refusal, he walked towards Helen.

15

After a few seconds, I glanced round. Danny and Helen were standing together, embracing, kissing. Naked.

I noticed that Simon was also watching them, although he still hadn't moved.

'Can I have my clothes?' I asked.

'Say "please".'

'Please can I have my clothes?'

'No,' said Simon. Then he added: 'But you can have this.'

His wet costume hit the beach a few feet in front of me. He sprang over the breakwater, landing almost as close. He stood without moving, just a shadow against the breakwater.

'You're lovely,' he said, softly – and I realized he could see much more of me than I could of him.

I didn't like Simon staring at me, slowly inspecting my nude body, so I moved towards him to restrict his view. He took that as an invitation, and he leaned forward, his lips pressing against mine, his mouth opening, his tongue optimistically thrusting forwards.

I raised my arms to fend him off, but that left me unprotected, and his hands homed in on my bare breasts. I gasped in astonishment. It was the first time I had ever been touched there, flesh to flesh, and it felt . . . very strange, but also very nice.

Instead of pushing Simon away, I found myself pulling him close to me. His hands dropped from my boobs and went around my back. His naked male flesh was warm, and I tingled all over at his touch. He was still trying to kiss me, but I turned my mouth away from him. Apart from that, our bodies were in total contact.

There was something pressing hard against my stomach, and I reached down to push it away. I obviously wasn't thinking, or I would have known exactly what it was.

I touched it. Warm and rigid. I let go immediately, because I now realized what it was.

It was Simon's penis.

Engorged with blood, swollen and vertical.

This was his hard-on. His cock, his dick, his knob, his prick, his tool . . .

Although I knew the theory of erection, this was the first time I had any practical experience.

Simon held his hips hard against my body. Even when I leaned back, he continued thrusting forward. Half a minute ago, I'd avoided studying that area of his body. Now I tried looking down, but there was nothing that I could see. Our bodies were too close. There was only one way that my curiosity could be satisfied. My heart beating faster than ever, I reached down again.

My fingertips touched Simon's cock, and once more they quickly withdrew. A few seconds later, my fingers returned, feeling the strength of his masculinity. We looked at one another, our eyes meeting for the first time. Simon remained still as I took hold of his prick, grabbing it in my palm, feeling it pulse with life, amazed at its size.

Then Simon closed his eyes, and his pulse suddenly became stronger. The warm male flesh began to twitch. Simon groaned.

I felt warm, wet spurts of spunk squirting onto my flesh.

I was both repulsed and fascinated. It was me who had caused this to happen, I realized. It was because of my body that Simon had ejaculated, and in that way I felt honoured.

'I'm sorry,' said Simon, pulling away. 'I'm sorry.'

He was smiling, however. He wasn't really sorry, and neither was I.

I gazed down at the silvery streaks on my skin, at the thick drops which rolled down my stomach towards my pubic hairs. More semen covered my

17

hand, and I rubbed my fingers together, sensing its unfamiliar texture.

The cloud which had been hiding the moon rolled away, and for the first time I could see Simon's cock. Now that it was spent, he was beginning to lose his erection. I wished I'd examined his knob more thoroughly when I had the chance – but I guessed there would be plenty more chances.

I raised my right hand, studying the silvery moonlit streaks. My left hand touched my stomach, feeling Simon's libation, rubbing it into my pubic hairs, and my fingers slid lower, lower . . .

I quickly drew my hand away, saying: 'I think I need another swim. How about you?'

Simon nodded. We glanced towards Helen and Danny, but they were lost in their own intimate explorations.

I began walking towards the sea. Simon followed, and I felt his eyes studying my naked body. I turned and walked backwards, so we could both look at one another as we went down the beach. We waded into the water together. He took hold of my right hand, then my left, and pulled me close to him. Our fingers were glued together with his spunk, and so was our flesh when our groins touched. I allowed him to kiss me. We'd done this before, when we'd been part of the under-the-pier gang, but for the first time he seemed to know what he was doing.

'What about tomorrow?' Simon asked, after an eternity.

'What about it?'

'Same time? Same place?'

'For a swim, you mean?' I asked – but I reached down and caressed his prick, letting him know that wasn't what I meant.

At my touch, his tool immediately began to harden and ascend.

18

I laughed and sprang away, diving into the dark waters.

I knew it was going to be an interesting summer.

Chapter Two

Before we could return to the beach, however, we had a whole day to get through – and all four of us were in the same class for most subjects. Danny kept smirking, and I wondered if he'd been boasting to all his mates. I wasn't quite sure what he could have boasted about. How far had he and Helen gone last night? We hadn't yet discussed our nocturnal activities, but she'd spent most of the day smiling.

Simon, however, seemed as reticent and shy as ever. We said nothing to each other all day, but I suppose neither of us was very interested in what the other had to say. Our communication the previous evening hadn't really been on the verbal level, and we both knew it would be the same that night.

I couldn't wait for it to get dark, when I could get my hands on Simon's cock again.

'Stop dreaming, girl!'

I blinked and stared up at the woman looming over my desk. It was Miss Slatter, the geography teacher. Slatter the Slag, as she was known. Before it got dark, however, school had to finish. There were only two more lessons to get through. After geography came economics with Miss Booth, better known as Booth the Bag. The two subjects I hated most. Or, more precisely, the two teachers I hated most.

'Fuck you, Miss,' I muttered and looked down at the map in front of me.

When Slatter turned and waddled away, I looked out of the window. The sun was shining, and the sea was only a mile away. I couldn't wait for the holidays. When I came back next term, I'd be concentrating on maths and science. There would be no more geography, no more economics. No more Slag, no more Bag.

When I finally called for her that evening, Helen asked: 'What time were we there last night?'

'I don't know,' I said. 'Eleven o'clock, was it? But we don't have to be there at exactly the same time.'

'It's probably best to be late, so they don't think we're too eager . . . '

' . . . even if we are!'

We both laughed.

'I never really thought much of Danny before,' said Helen. 'But he's very good-looking, isn't he?'

He wasn't – which was why Helen had never thought much of him before. Danny was very average, in appearance as well as everything else. There was nothing which made him more distinctive than most of the boys in school. The same was true of Simon, which was why I hadn't previously paid him much attention, but now I was thinking about him all the time. Or, more precisely, I was thinking about one particular part of him. Maybe that was it. Helen and I were both mesmerized by our first real sexual encounters.

I was fairly sure that Helen was as sexually inexperienced as I was, at least until last night – despite her claim of *I know what I'm doing*. If she'd ever done more than I had, I'd have heard all about it. We spent so much of our time together that she hadn't had much opportunity to do something of which I was unaware; and perhaps it was because we were together so much that we both had so little contact with the male of the species. Several other girls in our class boasted about how many times they'd fucked, and they graphically compared their experiences. A lot of it was exaggeration, but a lot wasn't.

I was so innocent. Allowing a boy to fondle my boobs had seemed very daring, although I'd never allowed one to slip his hand inside my blouse. Then

21

last night Simon had touched my bare tits, which had been a sudden advance. We'd been naked together. I'd held his prick. And he'd spurted his hot seed all over me.

It had been quite an evening, little wonder that it had taken me so long to fall asleep that night. It was the heat which kept me awake, I'd thought, as I lay in bed. I was naked, the covers pushed away. But the heat was inside me, I discovered. I kept remembering what had happened, going over and over it again in my mind. Remembering Simon's hands on my breasts, I'd stroked my boobs, feeling the hardness of my nipples against my palms. I rubbed the taut skin of my stomach, imagining it was still sticky with Simon's sperm, and I found my fingers exploring my pubic curls, pressing down hard on my pelvic bone, feeling a strange sensation deep within, a craving which I didn't know how to satisfy. The only way that my yearning could be appeased, I thought, was to have something deep inside me. That meant only one thing: I was a woman, and I wanted to fuck.

'Fuck,' I'd whispered, and for the first time ever I was using the word in its anatomical sense, not as an obscenity. 'Fuck, fuck, fuck, fuck, fuck . . . I want to *fuck*. I want to be *fucked*. I want a *cock* in my *cunt*. I want, I want . . . '

The idea was both exciting and scary. I was well aware that I didn't know what I really did want. Perhaps too much had happened all at once, or perhaps not enough. Maybe if Simon hadn't ejaculated so quickly, I'd have been swept along by the overwhelming sexual tide which had begun to engulf me, and allowed him to slide his prick deep within me. That would have solved a lot of things, and I wouldn't need to worry about 'the first time' any more.

When we headed back up the beach after our swim, Simon had another hard-on. His knob thrust upwards, asserting its virility, and he made sure that I was aware of the fact. But by then the moment was gone – for me, if not for him. All I wanted was to get dry and dressed, and all I wanted from Simon was to borrow his towel.

'Tomorrow,' I'd assured him. 'Same time. Same place.'

The following night, I had my own towel. Helen was even better equipped, because she carried a blanket in her beachbag.

'Might as well be comfortable,' she told me. 'I don't want sand up my bum. Or up anywhere else.'

It was evident that Helen thought we would be going through a similar procedure as last night. I assumed we'd be able to dispense with the preliminary formalities, the process of undressing and getting naked. In that case, why was she wearing her best clothes?

I didn't bother to ask. I simply waited while she finished combing her hair and putting on her make-up. No one would see her make-up in the dark, and I guessed that her hair would soon become tangled as she rolled about on the beach.

Finally, we headed off for our after-dark swim . . . and moonlit grope.

I realized that I was very nervous. What if Simon and Danny weren't there? But so what? We could still go for a swim.

'Should we go for a drink first?' I suggested, thinking that alcohol might calm me down.

'No, let's get it over with.'

'You make it sound like going to the dentist.'

Helen forced a laugh, and it sounded like a forced laugh. She felt as uneasy as I did. I guessed that she had spent so long getting ready because that was her way of delaying our arrival at the beach. When we got there, however, it was evident from the height of the tide that we were early. But so were Simon and Danny.

23

'Hi.'

'Hi.'

'Hi.'

'Hi.'

The boys were leaning against the breakwater, and we all looked at each other. The moment grew longer and longer, and still nothing happened. I was wishing I was somewhere else, and I assumed that the other three were wishing the same. There was somewhere else that we could go, and I said:

'Who's for a swim?'

They all looked at me, but no one answered.

Helen was all dressed up. I wasn't. I was wearing a T-shirt, shorts and sandals. So I peeled off my top, turning away as I did so. And I mean that I was wearing a T-shirt, shorts and sandals: I had nothing on underneath.

No bra, no briefs, I was ready for anything. Or nothing. But the night wouldn't be wasted. I was going swimming, no matter what. I kicked off my sandals, thumbed down my shorts, and walked towards the sea. I felt three pairs of eyes watching my naked body. All they could see was my bare behind; but when I returned, they'd be able to see far more.

By the time I reached the water's edge, Simon had caught up with me. He'd also stripped off. The first thing I noticed was his cock – it was erect, of course. We waded into the sea together.

'We must be mad,' said Simon.

I presumed he was referring to the temperature of the water, and I tended to agree.

'Think how great it will be when we come out again,' I said.

Simon looked me up and down, and he smiled. 'I hope so,' he said.

'That's not what I meant,' I told him, and I splashed him with water. 'You need cooling down. Or part of you does.' And it was that part of his anatomy at which I was aiming.

He tried kicking a spray of sea-water at me, but I sprang away and leapt into the ocean. Simon plunged in after me, and we swam up and down for several minutes, never more than a few yards apart. Whenever he tried to outdistance me, I kept pace with him. His technique wasn't very good, he wasted a lot of unnecessary energy, and I could easily have pulled away. That didn't seem advisable, however. I was only a girl, and he wouldn't be too pleased if I showed him up.

When he tried chasing me through the water, I didn't try too hard to get away. I let his hands find my body, stroking my thighs and rubbing my breasts, but then I kicked away from him again. I didn't want to make it too easy for him – or for him to think that I was too easy.

Helen and Danny remained on the beach, lost in the darkness. In the distance we could hear a few other people in the sea. Water magnified sound, and it seemed they must have been swimming near the pier. Probably some of them were in our class, I thought; but they were probably all wearing costumes.

Simon and I looked at each other, tacitly agreeing that it was time to head back to the beach. We swam towards the shallows and stood up – although I noticed that a certain part of Simon was not standing up.

'The cold makes it shrink,' he commented, looking down at his wilted penis.

'It has the opposite effect on me,' I remarked, as I fingered my hardened nipples.

'And this is the effect you have on me,' he said.

Sea-water dripped from his moonlit flesh, but his manhood was visibly lengthening, stiffening, growing. The transformation was amazingly fast, changing

25

him from a little boy to a rampant stud in a matter of seconds.

It was all because of me. This was the first time I had witnessed the full phenomenon, and the effect that a female can have upon a male has always seemed mysterious and magical. A man's sexuality is so blatant, there is no way that his interest can be disguised. But the effect a male can have on a female is equally as powerful, although expressed in a far more subtle fashion, and my pulse was already speeding when Simon's arms embraced me.

He pulled my nude body against his wet torso, and I felt his rigid cock pressed up between us. It was the warmest part of his whole body. His hands found my buttocks, caressing them. My hands stroked his back, his thighs, then settled for rubbing his firm behind. We kissed, long and hard, our tongues taking it in turns to venture into each other's mouth, then retreating, forced back as the invading tongue began to explore the other's mouth. My heart was racing by now, and my limbs felt weak.

Simon removed one of his hands and, although our lips remained locked together, he leaned away slightly. His palm slipped up between our ribs and cupped my right breast, the fingers encircling my nipple. It had been firm because of the cold water, but now it became even harder.

I gasped at his touch, and drew my mouth away from his. Misunderstanding my reaction, Simon started to pull away from my breast. I grabbed his wrist, directing his hand back to where I wanted it, and I gazed down as his fingertips teased my nipple between his thumb and forefinger. I was sure the nipple had never been larger.

'What's wrong with the other one?' I whispered, and I nodded down to my other bare boob.

Simon said: 'How about . . . ?'

He could say no more, because a moment later his

mouth was too busy. His lips descended upon my left breast, and I felt his tongue licking lightly at the nipple.

I shuddered with delight. The touch of his tongue was exquisite, and I closed my eyes, denying one of my senses so that I could enjoy the others more: the sound of my own heavy breathing, the taste which lingered of Simon's kiss, the scent of the fresh breeze, and, more than anything, the absolute bliss of having my nipple sucked.

I never realized that any part of my body could be so sensitive. The nipple had dilated totally, even the areola swelling above the flesh of my breast.

We were still standing in the water, the sea slowly retreating as the tide went out. I lost all track of time as Simon introduced me to a whole new world of sensation. I pressed my stomach against his hard cock, sliding my hips from side to side and up and down, feeling his hot male flesh rub against my bare skin. My hands were on his buttocks, forcing him against me.

By now Simon was fondling my left breast, licking my right – and it kept feeling better and better. It was as if he were stroking and licking me all over, that he was rolling his engorged penis over every inch of my eager flesh. He kept on taking me to greater heights, leading me to a place I had never been before except in my dreams.

I sensed a warmth building up deep within, a glowing incandescence which was at the centre of my being.

I shifted my feet on the sand, still beneath the water, and I parted my legs slightly. I was so hot there, at the junction of my thighs, and so damp – but the wetness was not caused by my swim. It was caused by something else entirely . . .

Simon's lips were still engulfing one of my nipples, his fingers still caressing the other. Then he finally made use of his free hand. I felt his fingers low on my stomach, moving down through my pubic hairs. I became still, but he did not. His hand moved closer and closer to the most intimate part of my body. It was what I wanted, what I needed and desired, but it was also so alien to be touched there.

My social conditioning overcame my primeval instinct, and I found myself stepping back out of reach. I was panting heavily, my nipples wet with Simon's saliva, and I took a deep breath. I shivered for a moment, suddenly cooling down as my internal fires were extinguished.

'What's the matter?' he asked.

I shook my head. 'Nothing,' I said – and I didn't know if it was the truth or a lie.

'Is there anything I can do? Anything you want?'

I glanced at his cock, which was still as hard as ever, and I smiled. I wanted to see his geyser blow.

'Yes,' I told him.

'What?

'Do what you did last night.'

In the moonlight, I saw Simon frown, not knowing what I meant. A second later, his expression changed as he suddenly realized, and he glanced down at his erection. 'You mean . . . ?'

I nodded.

'Here? Now?'

'Yes,' I replied. 'Yes.'

He glanced around, and I became aware how vulnerable we both were. We stood naked where the sea turned to shore, clearly visible to anyone in the vicinity. It was very late, but that meant little. There were often people on the beach. People going for a midnight stroll; people taking their dogs for a walk; people fishing; even other people swimming.

Half a minute later, I had been oblivious to everything except the effect of Simon's attention upon my body. I wouldn't have cared if I'd been naked in the

28

shopping centre at noon, being fondled and caressed in full view of the whole town.

'Do it,' I told him.

'It isn't that simple,' he said. 'It won't do it on its own.'

'It did last night.'

'It usually needs – er – a hand.' As he spoke he ran his fingertips up the length of his shaft, then back again. He cupped his balls, seeming to weigh them in his palm, then gripped his cock between his thumb and forefinger. Then he added: 'I'll let you watch me, if I can watch you.'

'Watch what?' I asked. 'You are watching me.'

'That's not what . . . okay, you can be my inspiration. Don't stand so far away.'

I moved closer. But not, I told myself, because Simon had asked. I wanted to be nearer so I could see better.

Once again, Simon glanced around. 'It's a bit exposed here, isn't it?'

'Do it.'

'You're a bossy bitch.'

'Yeah,' I agreed.

He shrugged. 'I'm not used to an audience, but . . .'

Then he sank down onto his knees, stretching out until he lay on his side along the edge of the sea. Propped upon his left elbow, he was half covered in water, the waves lapping across his body and then receding.

His eyes were focused on me as his hand started sliding up and down his penis, up and down.

I watched, my heart beating faster and faster, seeming to keep time with the rhythm of Simon's masturbatory strokes.

I felt very isolated standing up. If anyone had been watching, they would only have been able to see me. Simon seemed to have sunk almost out of sight – except I could see him. But if I also lay down, I'd be able to see even better. I knelt near him, then sat down, the waves washing up against my hips.

'Don't look so serious,' he said. 'I'm enjoying myself, even if you aren't.'

Drawing my gaze from his hand and his knob, I noticed that Simon was smiling.

'But I am,' I assured him – and I was. I smiled, hoping to prove it.

Simon seemed quite content to have me watching. I was uneasy as a voyeur, although maybe it was my position which was less than comfortable. I felt that I had to play my part in what was happening. The least that I could do was join him, my position mirroring his. I lay on my side opposite Simon, propping myself up on my right elbow. We were about two feet apart, the dark waves washing between us.

I gazed at Simon as he stroked his manhood, while he gazed at me. My left hand reached out, caressing him almost at random; stroking his face and his thighs, rubbing his hair and his chest. Meanwhile, his right hand was moving faster and faster.

Less than a minute had passed since he began wanking, when he announced: 'You wanted it. Here it is.'

I slid closer to him, through the sand and the sea, and I said: 'Do it over me.'

The previous night it had happened almost without my realizing, but discovering Simon's spunk spurting onto my naked flesh had given me a great thrill. Now I wanted to watch as he ejaculated – and again I wanted him to come over me.

He did. Simon aimed his cock towards me, and suddenly a moonlit streak of spunk jetted from the end of his quivering knob. It squirted through the darkness, travelling much further than I could have imagined, and landed between my breasts. I gazed down at Simon's offering, mesmerized. Half a second later there was another flash of quicksilver, and more sperm splattered on my flesh. Then came another glittering arc, followed by another.

Each spurt was less forceful, travelling less distance and being less substantial, but each was a bonus. I'd assumed that there was but one ejaculatory gush, not a whole series of pulses.

I gazed down at my nude torso, at the streaks of hot semen which dripped from my breasts and flowed down across my flesh. I rolled onto my back, using both of my hands to massage the male essence into my skin as if it were some expensive body lotion. But as the salt waves rippled over me, I found myself rubbing the water over my flesh, unsure whether I was trying to mix it with Simon's spunk or to wash it away.

'Same time,' said Simon, smiling, 'same place?'

The moon was low on the horizon, almost full, and wisps of dark cloud drifted lazily across its golden orb. The sky was aglow with millions of stars. And on one insignificant world, the ocean flowed over my body, up between my parted legs, then over my thighs, between my breasts and through my hair. I lay on my back as the waves receded, like a mermaid cast ashore by the tide.

I managed to turn my head towards Simon. The first thing I noticed was his dick, which now hung wilted and spent, no longer of any interest to me. But there was always tomorrow.

'Well . . . ?' asked Helen, as we finally made our way home.

'Well what?' I asked.

'What happened? That's what!'

'We went for a swim. Did you?'

I knew that Helen hadn't been swimming. Her hair was still dry. And if she and Danny had headed for the ocean, Simon and I would have known about it.

It seemed that the two of them had spent all their time beneath Helen's blanket.

'No,' said Helen.

'You should have done,' I told her. 'It was great.'

'So was what I was doing with Danny.'

'Really? So was what Simon and I did – and we also went swimming . . . '

Helen laughed, and she suddenly put her arm around me. She pulled me close, kissing my cheek.

'Hey!' I said, pulling back and making a show of wiping my face.

'Just feeling randy,' she told me.

'Lesbian!' I muttered, then I laughed.

This was something we had both joked about in the past. If we'd never had real boyfriends, and if we spent so much of our time together, did that mean we were lesbians?

It was just a word. We knew as little about lesbianism as we did about fucking. No, that wasn't quite true. We were both female, so we were both aware of our inherent sexuality – while we knew nothing of the male. Until last night. And tonight.

But now, it seemed, I knew more about male sexuality than my own.

What had Helen been doing? I was sure that her evening couldn't have been as interesting as mine. What could she have done with her clothes on?

Then I realized that very few girls could have gone through such a swift initiation as I had done. Being naked saved a lot of trouble. All that fumbling with clothes, unhooking and unzipping. Our ancestors never had to bother with that kind of stuff. What Simon and I had done last night had been a first for me, and probably for him; but the same kind of thing had happened to countless millions before.

It was a simple equation: male plus female equals ejaculation.

It could happen while fucking, with cock in cunt.

It could happen while just fooling around.

But in that case it could lead to a lot of sticky stuff all over the clothing. Being naked saved all that, and being naked by the sea saved even more – it was easy to wash off my bare flesh.

Things were happening fast between me and Simon. He didn't have to undress me before sucking my tits, because I'd already been naked.

I knew, however, I'd been somewhat inhibited in what I'd done on our second night together. The previous evening I'd twice touched Simon's cock, the first time in surprise, the second in admiration. But tonight I seemed to have made no contribution except allowing him to do what he wanted, to fondle and suck my boobs.

That was what he wanted; but it was also what I wanted. And then he'd obeyed my instructions to jerk himself off – which was also what he wanted.

I found myself studying Helen's clothes, looking for signs of semen, or where she had wiped away Danny's come. There was no trace of anything. Her clothes were a bit creased, but unstained. I wondered what they had been doing together all that time, but I didn't want to ask.

'And did Danny enjoy himself?' I asked.

'I heard no complaints . . . '

'Uh-huh.'

' . . . just heavy breathing.'

'Uh-huh.'

'And Simon?'

'Uh-huh.'

We walked on, then looked at each other, both wanting to ask an infinity of questions but not knowing where to begin. We had been best friends for most of our lives, but now something had separated us. Boys. Men. Sex.

'What do they want, Helen?' I asked.

'To fuck us.'

'That's what I thought.'

And we both laughed again.

'But before that?' I asked.

'They want,' Helen said, 'us to do to them what they do to us.'

'What? Lick their tits?'

Helen laughed so much that she had to stop walking.

'No,' she finally managed to say, shaking her head as she still laughed. She lifted her right hand and wiggled her index finger. 'They do this to us.' She made her hand into a fist, and she jerked it up and down. 'And we do this to them.'

I realized that Helen had just given me my programme for tomorrow night.

Chapter Three

But there was the rest of that night to get through before tomorrow.

When I arrived home, I went up to my room and stripped off. I stared at my nude self in the full-length mirror. My whole body was slightly pink as if with the first traces of sunburn; but unlike when I'd been on the beach in previous years, there was no bikini line. Every inch of my flesh was tingling. And I was also aglow inside, thinking of the time I'd spent with Simon, of what had happened, what might have happened – and what might happen next.

I ran my hands over my skin, cupping my breasts, lightly squeezing my nipples between my fingers. Then I ran my palms between my boobs and further down my chest, where Simon's sperm had spurted over me. Despite washing it away in the ocean, I could almost still feel his come on my flesh. I raised my right hand to my face, and lightly licked my fingertips, tasting the salt of the sea.

But my skin was damp with sweat, so maybe it was myself that I could taste – or maybe it was the lingering taste of Simon . . .

I watched my naked image in the mirror, as my left hand kept moving lower, down over the flatness of my stomach and then venturing between my pubic curls. It was as if it were someone else's hand which was exploring such forbidden territory.

My awareness felt completely different. In some ways it was almost like being drunk, when everything was distorted and exaggerated; and I was enjoying myself, calm and relaxed as if inebriated. But in other ways, the sensations I was experiencing were the exact opposite because I was fully aware both mentally and physically. My senses were heightened by sexual intoxication.

I noticed that my index finger was curled, exactly as Helen's had been.

'They do this to us,' she had said. 'And we do this to them.'

She had been describing what had happened to her earlier, what she and Danny had been up to. She must have jerked him off, and then he'd slipped his finger between her legs . . .

And that was what Simon had wanted to do to me. I hadn't allowed him to touch me, although now I imagined that it was not my finger which was probing the unknown, but Simon's. I could feel my heart beating faster, my pulse increasing as the blood raced through my veins.

Then suddenly I stopped, and my left thumb joined my index finger to tug at what it had discovered within my blonde curls – a tiny frond of seaweed!

I laughed, then went for a shower and to wash my hair. I washed my hair first, rinsed out the shampoo, then squeezed a pool of conditioner into my palm. It looked just like spunk, I thought. It was almost the same colour and texture, although not so warm. I smiled at the idea as I rubbed my hands together, smearing the slimy liquid across my palms and between my fingers, then I worked it into my hair and scalp.

I stood under the shower, allowing the hot spray to flow across my body, and I began to soap myself. As I did so, I remembered the touch of Simon's hands on my bare flesh. I soaped my buttocks, and remembered how it had felt when Simon had stroked my buttocks; I soaped my breasts, and remembered how it had felt when Simon had stroked my breasts. My nipples became even harder at my touch. My fingers lingered on the delicate pink flesh, and I felt a new warmth radiate throughout my whole body. I'd touched my breasts countless times before without producing such an effect. But that was perhaps because I had never caressed myself in such a way. The physical sensation was magnified by the mental image of Simon's hands fondling my bare boobs.

Standing under the hot shower was normally very relaxing, but not in this instance. Instead of slowing down, my pulse was still racing. Needles of hot spray cascaded off my back and coursed across my buttocks and over my thighs. I gazed down at myself, seeing my breasts rise and fall as I breathed in and out, watching as I lazily lathered my ripe flesh.

My right hand slid lower, vanishing through the swirling steam. I recalled how wet and sticky I had become down there, and realized that I needed to pay special attention to the junction of my thighs. I soaped my pubic hairs more thoroughly than ever, and each time my fingers moved slightly lower – and each time I could feel my temperature increase. It was nothing to do with the hotness of the shower, I knew. Even if it had been an icy cold spray, the fires deep within my body would have kept on raging.

I turned, letting the hot spray splash across my face and breasts, and drip down my ribs and stomach, down to where my right hand was still slowly descending. But then it could go down no further; the index finger had to turn, following the curve of my pubic bone.

Then I touched what I had never touched before. There it was, hidden between the folds of my swollen labia.

I knew its location, because I'd read about it so often, but until tonight I'd never had any real need for it.

I discovered my clitoris.

And I gasped as my fingertip touched the sensitive flesh.

37

I withdrew quickly, as if I had burned myself.

But the feeling was the exact opposite of pain – a shudder of absolute pleasure had flowed throughout my body now that I had finally found the heart of my femininity. I wanted to touch myself again, for more than a brief instant this time, and part of my being craved that caress; but also I wanted to wait, to save such intimate attentions until later, when my desire would be even more insatiable.

It was as if I thought it was some luxury which could only be consumed once, like an expensive cake or a liqueur chocolate. I would enjoy it all the more the longer I waited, the eager anticipation being all part of the process.

This was true, I have since discovered. Sex is more than screwing. The build-up is also important. The moment that I meet a new guy, I always wonder if I'm going to end up fucking; and I even fantasize about men I see casually, in the street or in a bar. Without exchanging a word, without even giving him a second glance, I can have him stripped naked and shafting me.

One of the best moments is when you both *know* that you are going to fuck. You might realize it almost as soon as you have met, and it might take a long time before it ultimately happens. Or the relationship might develop more slowly, as you begin to notice someone more and more, and you both finally become aware that you will end up fucking each other crazy. But, for me, the time you really become lovers is when you both accept the inevitable – the fact that you *will* fuck.

Then comes the period of anticipation, which can last as long as it takes you both to tear off your clothes, or it can go on much longer. You can let him think he is seducing you. You can play hard to get, although perhaps not too hard to get. But it's all part of the process, the different moves each of you makes, the different signals you give to one another. The scheming, the planning, the plotting, they're all part of the fun.

My first experiences of sex were on the beach with Simon, when I was already naked. It took me a while to discover the pleasures of dressing for a potential lover, of wearing glamorous clothes and exotic lingerie. The whole reason for wearing such garments was so that they could be removed by me – or by him.

Perhaps because of how I started out, or perhaps because of my profession, I've always found it very daring *not* to take off my clothes. To be fucked with my skirt up around my waist, or my jeans around my knees has always seemed specially stimulating . . .

The anticipation is great, imagining how a new lover will perform, wondering what kind of tricks he likes to do – and have done to him. And when you finally fuck, that isn't the end. It's only the beginning, because you can do it again and again and again.

That was my mistake as I stood in the shower. I must have believed that I could only have one taste of the luxury I'd been offered. But sex wasn't like a cake or a chocolate, that once it was eaten it was gone. A fuck led to another fuck.

It might not occur immediately, however, because of a basic design fault in the male anatomy: after ejaculation, they usually lose their erections – and a limp dick is no use to any woman. As far as I'm concerned, a man *is* his cock. Without a hard-on, he's of very little use to me. He can use his fingers, use his tongue, even use some kind of artificial appliance. They can be great, but I'm a simple girl, I like simple things: I like fucking.

I've tried most sexual activities, and enjoyed most of them. I like variety and variation, but my favourite activity is still the most plain and simple of them all. One girl, one guy: that's the perfect equation. One cunt plus one prick equals absolute bliss. It takes a lot to beat an energetic tool sliding in and out of my eager twat.

Women have a great advantage over men: we can achieve orgasm after orgasm, reach peak after climactic peak. Without a shadow of a doubt, to be a female is to be the sexiest of the sexes.

The first time I touched my clit, this was something of which I was unaware – the fact that I could keep on touching myself without diminishing my pleasure. In fact, the opposite was the case.

I reached up for the shower-head, holding it in one hand as I rinsed the soap from my body. Hot water jetted over my torso and legs, and then I bent my head and directed the spray at my hair, washing out the conditioner. As I leaned forward, I noticed that there was one area of my anatomy that I had missed rinsing. My pubis was still covered in bubbles of lather. I finished doing the hair on my head first – then aimed the spray at my pudenda.

I was still very hot, burning up from within, and the water couldn't quench my inner heat. The fires flared even more. When I had rinsed away the last of the soap, I reached for the tap. But instead of turning off the water, I increased the pressure. The needles of spray hit my pelvic mound with greater force than ever. I parted my legs, aiming the shower directly upwards. The jets splashed against my hidden flesh, and I closed my eyes, luxuriating in the unique sensation.

Words like 'orgasm' and 'climax' were still only dictionary references – except for Simon's spectacular eruptions over my naked flesh. I could feel myself climbing higher and higher, ascending towards an unknown peak; but there seemed to be some obstacle preventing me reaching the unconquered summit.

I moved the spray closer and closer towards my untamed cunt. My pulse was pounding, my breath coming in short bursts. I felt something touch my secret flesh, and I shouted out in surprise, then realized that I was rubbing the shower head across my most sensitive zone.

This was no use. I was too tense. I needed to relax, to be somewhere I felt more safe and comfortable. So I switched off the shower, climbed out, quickly dried myself – and went straight to bed.

I usually read at night, turning the pages until I became more and more tired. My favourite fiction was fantasy. I'm not talking about romantic novels, which I'm sure are total fantasy. I mean the real thing. Books set in the worlds of never, full of sorcerous adventures in fantastic realms of dark castles and evil wizards, of bold warriors and beautiful princesses. I knew that these epic tales were sneered at as escapism but what was wrong with that? In any case, they weren't very much different from movies and television series. To me, films about the rich and famous were even more remote and unrealistic than tales of demons and dragons.

I lay naked in bed, finding it hard to concentrate on the final volume of the trilogy which had kept me enthralled all month. I finally managed to get comfortable, holding the book in my left hand as I began to lose myself amongst the witches and warlocks. Not all of my attention was captured, however. Although my mind was caught up in the spell of wondrous words woven by the author, my body was still restless. As if obeying its own primal instincts, I became aware that my right hand was sliding down towards my vagina.

My cunt was already damp, the labia swollen, the clitoris erect.

And for the second time, I touched my clit.

It felt marvellous, and this time I did not immediately withdraw. My finger lingered on the delicate bud of flesh, stroking it lightly, sending waves of delight convulsing through my whole being.

41

I let the book drop from my grip and fall to the ground, giving up on the fantasy of fiction and surrendering my innocent cunt to the magical attention of my probing fingers.

One hand wasn't enough. I didn't know precisely where I should have been touching myself, and I was too impatient to find out. I needed total physical contact. My left hand joined my right, all of my fingers caressing and stroking my moist vaginal lips, feeling my clitoris grow even more, sensing the inner heat building up deep within. The more I touched myself, the hotter became the fires.

The incandescence raged more ferociously every moment, soon becoming an inferno which threatened to engulf every atom of my being.

My breath came in short bursts, faster and faster. My hips jerked upwards, meeting my hands, and my fingertips stroked the folds of sensitive cunt flesh, which became wetter every moment. My eyes were shut, my mouth wide open, and then without warning I suddenly gasped in ultimate ecstasy.

The experience was unbelievable. My whole essence was consumed by the eruption, and I was created anew from the embers. All I could do was sigh with total contentment. Every inch of my flesh was damp with sweat, and I needed another shower, but I had no intention of moving – ever.

An eternity passed before my body had ceased to quiver, until I was able to breathe again and my pulse returned to normal. All I could do was smile. I lay motionless in bed, aglow in the radiant aftermath of my first-ever orgasm.

'Not so tight.'

I loosened my grip.

'Not so fast.'

I slowed down.

'A regular rhythm, yes, that's it.'

My right hand slid up and down Simon's cock, while he whispered his instructions. We were on the beach, as ever, naked, as ever. We'd already been for our swim, after which we waded ashore and lay down together by the breakwater. Helen and Danny were on the other side, higher up the beach. They hadn't been in the water. It didn't take much to guess what they were up to.

Meanwhile, Simon and I were locked in a passionate embrace, our hands roving over each other's bodies, our tongues probing each other's mouths. He rubbed his cock against my stomach, while I rubbed my tits against his chest. He reached for my crotch, his fingers stroking my pubic hairs. That felt nice, very nice; but when he tried to venture even lower, I pulled away.

I didn't pull away too far, and a moment later I reached for his prick. It was hard, of course; it nearly always was. At first I explored his tool with my finger-tips. Until now, I had been too far away to see his erection properly or it had been too dark, or else Simon's hand had covered most of his tool while he was jerking himself off. But because of the exceptional brightness of the moon, I had a better view of his knob than ever, and for the first time I was able to examine it in detail.

Simon's cock was more intricate than I'd guessed. I ran my fingers lightly over his glans, then slowly down his length, foraged through his wiry pubic hairs, before exploring his testicles. I could feel the two separate egg-shapes within his scrotum, but then his balls tightened as I fondled them, and I moved my hand back upwards. The diameter of the shaft was slightly wider at the base than further up, I noticed as I circled it with my palm. I felt his pulse surging through his cock as I tightened my grip and started to slide my hand up and down.

That was when Simon had begun giving me my

lessons in masturbation. I soon caught on. Perhaps it was instinctive . . .

We were lying side by side, facing each other, supporting ourselves on our elbows. Simon reached out to stroke my breasts, his fingers encircling the nipples.

'Don't,' I told him.

'Why not?'

'Don't,' I said, and I let go of his cock.

He withdrew his hand immediately. Although I'd recently discovered how much I liked having my boobs caressed and the nipples gently teased, at that moment I didn't want any distractions. I took hold of Simon's knob again, and he rolled over onto his back, letting me have my way with him.

All my attention was focused on his cock, but when I glanced at his face I saw that he was grinning. He was also watching as my fingers manipulated his firm tool.

'Enjoying yourself?' I asked.

'Yes, thanks – but it could do with a bit of lubrication.'

Although my hand was apparently sliding up and down, in fact it was gripping exactly the same part of his cock. Simon's penile flesh was loose, sliding up and down on the shaft. As my hand jerked up, it pushed the free skin at the top of his prick, which rode up over his glans; as my hand jerked down, the skin was pulled back and the rounded head would appear again.

'What do you suggest?' I asked.

Simon slid out his tongue.

'Is that what you do?' I asked.

He nodded.

'Really?' I said. 'Show me. Go on, lick your dick.'

'Not that,' said Simon, and he slowly shook his head. 'Spit, I mean. You could use spit as lubricant.'

'Mine or yours?'

44

'Give me your hand,' he said, sucking up saliva from his throat.

'Uuuuhhhh! No thanks.'

I moved even closer to Simon, leaning over his hard cock. For the first time, I could smell the aroma of his aroused manhood. It was like some exotic spice, and I found myself wondering what it would taste like . . .

Then I opened my mouth, and allowed a trickle of saliva to fall from my lips onto the end of Simon's knob. It dribbled over the smooth dome and around the ridge below the glans. I heard him sigh with pleasure, his whole body rippling with contentment, and I wondered how long it would take before he ejaculated. Not too soon, I hoped, and I removed my hand.

'What's wrong?' he asked immediately. 'Why did you stop?'

I studied his expression, and I learned something new.

'Nothing,' I said, and I took hold of his penis again.

His cock was in the palm of my hand. And so was Simon. While I controlled his prick, I controlled him. That was the power which any female had over any male, which every woman had over every man.

My hand slid up and down Simon's warm male flesh, now slick with my saliva, and he was no longer lying still. His hips were gently rocking up and down in rhythmic counterpoint to my hand movements. It was as if he were fucking, that my hand was my cunt, my saliva was my vaginal juices.

I was still very close, and Simon reached out to touch me again. This time I did not protest as his fingers roamed across my breasts. He was building up towards his orgasm, I knew, and I could feel my own internal temperature steadily rising. But when he tried to slide his hand between my legs, I blocked his advance with my own left hand.

It seemed as if I were protecting my cunt with my

45

palm, but out of sight my middle finger had found my clitoris. I shuddered with pleasure. My index and third finger were pressed hard against my inner labia, while the middle finger stroked my clit. I felt it grow larger, wetter, and I caressed the bud of tender flesh at the same speed as my right hand was wanking Simon.

He was almost forgotten, however, as I closed my eyes and concentrated upon my own rapture. But then Simon suddenly gripped my right hand, forcing it to halt, and I knew that his climax must be imminent.

He had ejaculated over me twice before, but this time I was in control of his knob. If it didn't do as I wished, I could squeeze much harder, replacing pleasure with pain. I tugged at Simon's penis, making him do as I wished.

As I rolled away, I felt a tremor within the shaft which signalled impending orgasm. I sank down on my back. My left hand was frantically working on my hot twat, while my right kept pulling at Simon. His climax was mine. I had created it. Now I wanted it and needed it. I wanted him to come all over me again; I needed his seed; I craved his eruption against my wanton flesh.

I felt the first ejaculation splatter on my left breast, and I opened my eyes in time to see the creamy drops sparkle in the moonlight as they dripped from my nipple. I aimed Simon's prick lower, and the next fountain rained across my ribs, down my stomach and almost to my navel.

The spurts came in regular jets, I'd learned, and I knew I had less than a second until the next one. That one hit my left hand, which I hadn't moved out of range quickly enough. But the fourth burst was a direct hit on my pubis, which started to trigger off my own convulsions.

I abandoned Simon's cock. It was no longer any use to me, and neither was he, and he was immediately forgotten. Now it was my turn. I closed my eyes and all my attention was devoted to myself and my own primitive desires.

My right hand slid over my pubic hairs. My fingers were already damp with my saliva, and now they became even wetter with Simon's spunk. I remembered what he had said about lubricant, and I smeared the streaks of semen all over my labia and across my pulsing clitoris, mixing up the hot male juice with my own intimate secretions.

Meanwhile, my left hand was stroking my left boob, wiping the first spurt of semen over my breasts and dilated nipples. While I enjoyed myself in ultimate luxury, the world was mine, and I was the world. Although almost lost in lust, I became aware that I was not alone.

As I caressed my boobs and fingered my cunt, I realized that I was under observation – and that it was not only Simon who was watching me.

I opened my eyes, looking first at Simon. He was gazing at me in awe as I fingered myself. Even though he had just ejaculated, his cock was still hard. He was stroking it with his right hand, trying to give himself another climax.

Then I turned, looking up to the breakwater. Two heads were staring down at me. Helen and Danny were watching me.

And I didn't care.

In fact, it was even better that they were watching. To have them as an audience was even more stimulating than being alone. I watched all of them as I kept on finger-fucking myself, faster and faster, my hips bucking as my impending orgasm came closer and closer.

I touched my left hand to my lips, to blow Helen and Danny a kiss. But my fingers tasted odd, and for a moment I wondered what the sticky substances on my fingertips could be. Then I realized it was semen.

47

I rubbed my fingers all around my lips – then thrust out my tongue to savour the taste.

Simultaneously, I thrust the fingers of my right hand even deeper into my throbbing cunt.

And I cried out in rapture as I came.

And came.

And came.

Chapter Four

'I think we're doing something wrong,' said Helen.

'It seems to produce the right effect,' I said, and I rubbed my hands together, wiping imaginary spunk from my fingers.

She had been unusually quiet when we'd walked home together after my explicit display on the beach. Perhaps she thought I'd gone too far, and maybe she was jealous because I'd blatantly flaunted myself in front of Danny. Neither had she mentioned it subsequently, and I had also remained silent on the subject. How I had masturbated in front of her and the two guys never seemed an appropriate topic of conversation.

I wondered if I should have felt ashamed. Whenever I thought of what I'd done, I felt hot – but not through embarrassment. Instead, I began to get turned on again. It was an odd sensation, becoming sexually excited by something which I had done. But it wasn't only the thought of stroking my clit which aroused me, it was also the idea of having an audience to what should have been a very private act.

I'd watched as Simon wanked himself off, and doing that for one other person of the opposite sex didn't seem so bad. But to do it for three people, and one of those another girl . . .

. . . neither did that seem so bad, I realized!

I was always shy and didn't like to be noticed. Things had certainly changed very swiftly. It wasn't that I was on my way to being an exhibitionist – it seemed I already was one.

What I'd done had only been one step beyond being naked. When a guy is wanking, it is far more blatant than a girl doing the same. In fact, with a hand over her pubis a girl is less exposed than when she is naked – even though her fingers might be buried deep within her cunt.

But I'd gone a lot further than that, I suppose. Rubbing spunk across my flesh and licking it from my fingers wasn't very subtle. I hadn't done it for effect, however. It was what I craved at the time – and what I've craved ever since.

Now it was a few days later as Helen grinned and shook her right hand, also flicking away imaginary drops of sperm.

'That's not exactly what I mean,' she said, smiling as she examined her palm. 'That's what they get out of it – but what do we get out of it?'

I wasn't really sure what she meant, but I raised my right index finger, curved it slightly, and wiggled it to and fro.

'I can do that better myself!' said Helen, laughing.

I also laughed, although the only finger I'd ever had in my cunt was my own.

'We meet them on the beach, right?' Helen continued. 'But shouldn't the evening start earlier, somewhere else? I'm sure most girls don't get felt up or give their guys a wank for nothing.'

'I see,' I said, nodding.

We'd both previously been out on dates with other boys from school; they'd paid for the pleasure of our company – without getting that much pleasure in return. Heavy kissing, fondling and groping, but that was all. I'd never tossed one of them off by way of a payment. Simon, however, had been rewarded for nothing. He and Danny were getting us cheap. Cheaper than cheap; we were free. They'd never paid a penny for all the entertainment we had given them.

'They should wine us and dine us,' Helen continued. 'Take us out to see a film first, or to a nightclub

– or anywhere. Even going for a walk would be a novelty.'

'You want the romance.'

'Yeah, the flowers, the gifts!' Helen laughed again. 'I just want the evening to last more than five minutes!'

I joined in Helen's laughter, although in a way it didn't bother me that Simon had never bought me a thing. I was glad that he and I had skipped all the formalities. Starting off naked had saved a lot of time and all the unnecessary preliminaries, otherwise I'd never have done so much so fast. But maybe now it was time to backtrack, to be taken out and made to feel special.

There wasn't much opportunity for that kind of thing in our town; but, from then on, we took every opportunity that we could. If Simon and Danny wanted us to go on the beach with them, we insisted that we were taken out first. Helen always preferred to go somewhere expensive. The best part for me, however, was still when we reached the beach.

I always managed a swim, no matter what the weather or the state of the tide. Because of various adverse factors, however, it wasn't always possible to get my hands on Simon's cock. But whenever I reached home and my own bed, I always had the consolation of my cunt. I never tired of exploring my own body. Every night was a new voyage of discovery, a new orgasm . . . or two . . . or more.

I'd never slept better, never had more exciting or more stimulating dreams. And if I ever happened to wake up during the night, my increasingly expert fingers could soon make those dreams come true.

The nights became days, the days became weeks, and the weeks passed by until summer arrived. It was as if the first day of summer coincided with the start of the school holidays, which in turn meant the beginning of the tourist season. I could never understand why anyone wanted to come to our town for a holiday, particularly as it was always my ambition to leave. But for some people, the highlight of their year was spending a week or two in one of the seafront hotels.

During the summer, the town also filled up with foreign students who had come over to learn the language at one of the 'academies' which flourished for a few brief weeks every year. There were always fights between the local boys and their overseas counterparts. Meanwhile, international relations took on a different meaning down on the beach, where fraternization between the girls and boys of different nationalities meant there was hardly an inch of free space beneath the pier once the sun had set.

But there was no holiday for me that year. I had to take a summer job, working as a cleaner in one of the town's hotels. The hours were very long, the pay very little, and I hardly saw any sun. For the first time in my life, my skin was as pale at the end of the summer as at the beginning. Helen worked as a waitress in her parents' restaurant. She hated her job even more than I did, and she was paid even less. Simon and Danny were also working, and so I didn't see as much of the other three as I had done recently.

I usually only saw Simon in the evenings, and so having to work should have made little difference. But often I was too tired to go out after a weary day, and all I wanted to do was go home and go to bed – and sample the sensual delights which I could offer myself.

Probably I was getting bored with Simon. Wanking him off every night was beginning to grow a little tedious. I'd become much better at it, however, trying out various methods in order to improve my technique. I could make him ejaculate almost at my command, timing his orgasm by the way that I manipulated his tool. I could stroke him fast or slow, grip him hard or soft, could tease and tempt; but once I'd done everything and knew every millimetre of his flesh, my enthusiasm had waned.

I'd had Simon's spunk over almost every part of my body, although I'd been careful to keep his ejaculations away from my face. He was still enjoying himself and, to be fair, he kept trying to do something different. But there were limits beyond which I would not go.

He desperately wanted to touch my cunt, and I wouldn't allow that. It was mine, mine alone. I'd only just discovered my twat and was still investigating its latent potential. I didn't mind finger-fucking myself while he was watching, but I wasn't yet ready to share my vagina.

And that meant I didn't want to fuck. I suppose it wasn't exactly a question of not *wanting* – because in a way I did wish to make the transition from a girl to a woman.

Perhaps I didn't feel ready for that ultimate step. When I was ready for that first fuck, I'd know. If it had already happened with Simon, that would have been fine, it would have been over and done. But it was as if he believed he had the *right* to be the first to screw me. It wasn't up to him, however; it was up to me. I was the one who would make the decision, although I already expected that it wouldn't be a conscious choice.

It was not my mind which would decide when I first fucked; it was my body which would know when the time was right – and when the man was right.

Until then, I made do with Simon and his spurting spunk. I was using him, but it was a safe bet that he liked being used.

Even though we were all working, we always tried to get together at least one night of the week. We'd go for a few drinks, perhaps spend a few hours in a club, then head for the beach. As the town filled up with tourists and students, we'd had to move further and further away from the centre in order to find a quiet stretch of beach.

I was late arriving at the bar, but I wasn't the latest.

'Where's Helen?' I asked, as I sat down at the table.

'She can't make it,' said Danny. 'They're preparing for a wedding reception tomorrow.'

'Drink?' asked Simon, standing up.

'Yes. A beer and a brandy.' Then, knowing Simon, I added: 'In separate glasses!'

'So it looks like a threesome tonight,' said Danny, looking me up and down.

'Just keep dreaming,' I told him.

I knew that he'd had his eye on me for a long time. At first I thought it must have been because of my masturbationary exhibition, then I realized that it was simply because I was a girl. I was female, and that was good enough reason for him to fancy me. But I had to admit that I was curious about Danny's cock, perhaps because I'd never seen him naked except for that first night, when I hadn't been paying too much attention. He never stripped off and went swimming. Neither did Helen. They stripped off for a different reason and were always too busy with one another for a swim.

They had spied upon me and Simon, but for some reason we had never got around to creeping up on them to discover what they were doing. I suspected that Helen and Danny had been fucking for quite a while, but whatever someone else did was of little interest to me. I was an exhibitionist, not a voyeur . . .

'How was work?' asked Simon, as he gave me my drinks.

'Don't ask,' I replied. 'This is the first time I've ever looked forward to going back to school.'

We talked, we drank. We drank, we talked. It seemed odd that Danny was there without Helen. I half expected him to go home, but when Simon and I headed for the beach, Danny stuck with us.

'See you tomorrow?' Simon said to him.

'Trying to get rid of me?'

'Yes.'

Danny let fly with a slow-motion punch at Simon's jaw, and Simon ducked away with equal slowness.

'You don't mind if I come, do you?' Danny asked me.

'How can you come without Helen?' Simon asked. 'You going to jerk yourself off?'

Danny was still looking at me, and he smiled.

'Aren't we best friends, Simon?' he said. 'Haven't we always shared everything? Remember how we first met all those years ago, when I let you play with my football?'

It seemed that Danny meant it was time for Simon to repay that loan. And it was obvious what Danny wanted to play with: me.

I felt very angry with this, and was hoping that Simon would start an argument. Maybe there would even be a fight, a real scrap without punches being pulled. Two guys fighting over me! I began to get excited at the idea, and that was on top of the excitement I was already feeling. My mind might not like the idea of Danny treating me as something with which Simon could return an old favour; but my body was becoming quite aroused at the thought. My nipples had hardened, and I felt a familiar surge of heat deep inside my cunt.

I pretended that what was going on had nothing to do with me. Leaving Simon and Danny, I headed down the beach, and behind me I could hear them talking. I knew they were talking about me. I didn't go too far down the beach, otherwise I would have been out of sight in the darkness.

Then I undressed. I did it very slowly, knowing that their eyes were on me. They became silent as they watched me peel off my clothes and carefully drape them over the breakwater. I had been facing the sea, but now I turned towards the boys. Naked, I was silhouetted against the moonlit ocean: my legs spread, arms akimbo.

I stood like that for several seconds, then turned and slowly walked down towards the edge of the water, wading into the cool waves. I knew there was no way that Simon and Danny could have refused my invitation.

When I heard them charging down the beach, I smiled. I glanced around for a moment, watching as they stripped off their clothes while racing towards the sea – and towards me.

They splashed into the water, and I dived away. It became a race as they tried to catch me – and I let them do so, allowing the winner's hands to stroke my body before I kicked away and pulled free. Then I would slow down again, roll over onto my back, tempting them with visions of my breasts and my pubis floating above the surface. Again I was the prize, letting the fastest touch my inviting flesh for a few seconds, and then I would dive beneath the waves. This time they became the prey, and I had but one target.

Although it was night and very dark beneath the waves, I never had any trouble locating their cocks, tugging at their male flesh. And that was how I knew which of them was which. After so long, I could recognize Simon's prick by touch. The one which felt unfamiliar was Danny's. It was longer, thicker – and I couldn't wait until we got back onto the beach . . .

It was up to me to decide when we left the water. The boys wouldn't leave without me, although I knew that they were as eager as I was to head for the shore. I wanted to tease them for as long as possible, but I also wanted to delay our return to shore for my own sake. Although I was excited I was also nervous, not knowing what would happen when we reached the beach. Thinking of the unknown delights which lay ahead, however, aroused me even more.

Finally, I kicked towards the beach, stood up in the shallows and walked ashore. The boys were behind me, but I resisted the urge to turn around. I didn't want Danny to know how interested I was in him – or, more particularly, in his cock. My heart was beating faster than it had done for a long time, my mind aswirl with all kinds of ideas.

I made my way up the beach, and could feel two pairs of eyes staring at my naked body. I walked as slowly as possible, giving them more to look at, before I finally sat down, leaning back against the breakwater. Simon came and sat on my right, Danny on my left. They both sat very close, their shoulders and hips hard against mine. I stared straight ahead, pretending they were not there.

'Remember that video we saw last week?' said Danny.

'The one your brother thought he'd hidden?' said Simon.

'Yeah. The one with that girl and the two guys.'

'I remember.'

'Hot stuff, huh?'

'Very hot.'

'At first she pretended she didn't want anything to do with them.'

'She soon changed her mind.'

'And how! The way she sucked the first one's cock while the other one was screwing her.'

'Then they swapped around. The first man fucked her juicy cunt while the second one was fucking her in the mouth.'

'All that spunk.'

'Dripping from her lips and her twat.'

They both nodded slowly, and slowly they turned to face me.

'Which end do you want?' asked Danny. 'You want to fuck her first, while I give her a mouthful?'

I reached out with my hands. My right touched Simon's prick, my left touched Danny's, and I slid my fingers along each length of hard flesh.

'One girl's more than a match for any two cocks,' I said.

They both smiled.

'Particularly cocks this small,' I added – and it was my turn to smile.

My hands became fists as I took hold of each scrotum, squeezing them tighter, tighter, almost too tight, asserting my control.

'Any problems, boys?' I asked.

'No.'

'No.'

They shook their heads, very quickly.

'Good.'

I relaxed my grip, allowing my fingers to uncurl and move up their cocks. Until that moment I hadn't really known what would happen next, but now it was so obvious – and I proceeded to wank both Simon and Danny simultaneously.

I'd previously practised with my left hand on Simon's knob, and so I had no difficulty manipulating Danny's rigid flesh. With a dick in each hand, comparisons were easy, and Danny's penis was definitely longer and thicker than Simon's. Simon's had seemed big enough, and I'd often wondered how a girl was supposed to find enough room for so much hard cock in her cunt.

But now I thought about having one in my twat and one in my mouth . . .

I could feel my labia moistening at the idea, sensed my clitoris begin to dilate.

Meanwhile my fingers glided up and down the firm flesh on either side of me. My hands acted in unison, and I half wondered if I could produce simultaneous geysers of spunk. Then I would change rhythm slightly, one hand sliding up while the other slid down. It wasn't only the size of Danny's cock which was different, I realized: somehow it didn't feel the same as Simon's.

I turned towards Simon, leaning down, opening my mouth and allowing a trickle of spit to fall on the end of his knob. I watched as my hand pushed his flesh upwards, the foreskin hiding the glans for a moment, then revealing it again. It glistened with my saliva, and the first drop of semen oozed free from the slit at the very tip.

Then I directed my attention towards Danny and his swollen dick, studying it for the first time. In the dim light I could see that my fingers had not deceived me, because his knob really was bigger than Simon's. Not only that, but there was no loose skin to slide over the dome. My dribble of saliva dripped off the head, down the thick shaft and onto my fingers. Danny had no foreskin; he'd been circumcised. This was another first for me.

Until now, Simon and Danny had simply leaned against the breakwater, enjoying the intimate attentions which I was devoting to their erections. But while I was still staring at Danny's cock, he put his right hand on my left thigh, and his left hand reached out to my left breast, stroking my naked flesh with his right hand, massaging my nipple with his left.

The only way I could have prevented him doing this was by pushing him away, which would have meant removing my hand from his tool or from Simon's.

I didn't: I was enjoying what I was doing; I was enjoying what he was doing.

Then Simon began to fondle my right boob, to rub my left leg, and I felt my whole body tremble with pleasure.

Never had I been touched by four hands, and every

inch of my flesh was aglow. I closed my eyes, enjoying the unique sensation of so much physical attention.

My hands never stopped moving, however. Up and down they slid on Simon's beautiful prick; down and up they glided over Danny's handsome cock.

I felt a mouth on one breast, lips sucking at the hard nipple. A moment later, my other boob was similarly engulfed, a hot tongue flicking across the nipple. I loved having my tits licked, but until now this had always been one breast at a time. Having them both worshipped together was far more than twice as wonderful, and I felt myself spiralling upwards. I gasped with delight.

Instead of drying out in the warmth of the night, my nude body was becoming damp. My outer flesh was moist with sweat, my inner flesh moist with my feminine juices. Four hands were exploring my body, causing me to breathe very heavily, my pulse to increase. Sixteen fingers and four thumbs roved over my skin, daring to venture where only I had ever touched myself. Eager fingertips stroked my pubis, probed down towards my virginal cunt.

Instead of preventing this intrusion, I found myself spreading my legs, welcoming this invasion of my forbidden zone.

And I shuddered as for the first time ever fingers other than mine touched my twat, stroking my labia and caressing my clitoris.

Simon and Danny had not been entirely serious when they'd discussed fucking me simultaneously, but at that very moment they could have done exactly what they wanted with me. I wouldn't have cared, in fact I would have adored it. They were still sucking my tits, stroking my thighs, masturbating me while I jerked them off. I was so near sexual overload that if one of them had decided to screw me, while the other slid his delicious knob into my mouth, I would have willingly allowed it.

Right then, I wasn't precisely sure what was going on. At first I'd been sitting up, with the guys on either side of me, but somehow I was lying on my back, my whole body writhing in uncontrolled passion. All I knew was that I was rapidly approaching orgasm, and that for the first time I had not created my own climax: it had been done for me.

My hips jerked up and down, up and down, my breath came faster, faster, my whole being cried out for release before the unendurable pressure building up deep within could tear me asunder. And the only escape was to open my mouth wide, wide, and give vent to my rapture.

Everything else was forgotten, because there was nothing else. There was only me and my orgasm. We were the universe.

I cried out in ecstasy as I achieved my most spectacular orgasm ever, which just seemed to go on and on, each explosion setting off another and another, each more powerful than the previous one.

Then I collapsed, totally limp and drained. I lay still, allowing my body to recover from its wonderful ordeal.

'Are you okay?' I heard Simon say.

I nodded. It was all I could do.

Finally, I opened my eyes. I felt something on my face, and I lifted my hand to wipe it away. It was warm and wet and sticky. My face and hair were speckled with thick drops of semen. This was another first.

Simon was kneeling above me, gazing down. Danny was sitting on my other side, also watching me. They were both grinning.

I wondered which of them had ejaculated over me. That was what Simon usually did, because I usually hosed his spray of spunk over my nude body; it was my trophy for producing his climax.

There was more creamy sperm across my breasts, I

61

discovered. They had both spurted over me, and I regretted not seeing it. Watching an ejaculation always gave me a thrill – but I'd had plenty of thrills tonight. I'd been so engulfed by passion I hadn't even been aware that they had climaxed over me.

I wiped at my face and breasts, feeling the texture of both samples of spunk, wondering if it was possible to tell which of them had targeted my face. It didn't really matter, I supposed.

'Is there anything you want?' Simon asked.

I glanced from him to Danny. They were both still smiling.

'No.' I also smiled. 'I've had all I want.'

And I had – for a while . . .

Chapter Five

A week later, it was my turn to say I couldn't see the others that night. I'd been asked to work very late at the hotel and promised a bonus for doing so. I could have refused, headed down the beach and jerked off Simon, but that no longer had much appeal. Having gone as far as I wanted to with Simon, I chose to stay at work.

I hadn't seen him since our three-way wank, and I was in no hurry to do so. More particularly, it was Danny whom I was trying to avoid. What had happened had happened, and I certainly had no regrets – quite the opposite. But I didn't want my sexual education to continue in that direction. One girl plus two guys was the wrong kind of mathematics.

It had worked out that one time because it hadn't been planned. I knew in theory that a girl could easily satisfy two men. Okay, it was more than theory: I'd done it.

But three was certainly a crowd, and I didn't want to take it any further. I kept thinking of what the boys had said about watching a video, when the girl in the film had a cock in her cunt and one in her mouth. I should have been horrified at the idea, but discovered that I was more fascinated than repulsed. In fact, I realized, a girl could deal with more than two pricks at once. As well as her twat and her mouth, she had her hands.

Although I hadn't seen Simon, I'd seen Danny a few times. He tried inviting me out and he tried asking me back to his house, but I always refused. I knew he only wanted one thing from me – which was okay, because it was the same thing Simon already got from me each time, and which Danny had already had. But I'd have felt that I was cheating on both Simon and Helen if I'd agreed to see Danny.

All the same, I was tempted. Each time he asked, I found it harder to say no, and I suspected I would probably agree the next time.

I didn't like the idea of going back to Danny's house, because that was his home ground. The beach was neutral territory, and I always felt safe there – but I kept wondering if I wanted to feel safe, as I remembered the touch of male hands exploring my vulva and presenting me with that miraculous orgasm.

Simon had at last got his hands on my cunt, but I was certain that it must have been Danny who was the expert, who knew exactly where to feel me up. I knew how he had learned twat-touching and on whose clitoris and labia he had practised. Just as Simon had taught me how to stroke his cock, Helen had educated Danny in the seductive art of finger-fucking.

I could bring myself off whenever I wanted, but the idea of having someone else's finger on my trigger was in itself stimulating enough to make my cunt wet. Whenever I wanted, I knew, I could have Danny masturbate me. He might not want to stop at that, however, and neither might I.

I remembered how I had become so lost in the tides of my impending orgasm, that I hadn't cared what happened. While drowning in waves of pleasure, I'd have been helpless to stop Simon and Danny doing whatever they wished with my pliant body.

The same would have been true if Danny could bring me to such a peak that I craved a fuck. I'd want him to shaft me, I'd even need him to do so. But I didn't want to reach that stage – because Danny simply wasn't the one I wanted to claim my virginity.

Despite having said I wouldn't be able to join the other three, the extra work finished earlier than expected. I was tempted to go straight home, because I still had a valid excuse for not going out that night. The following day was my day off, however, and it seemed a waste to go to bed early if I didn't need to. The sea looked absolutely perfect for a swim, and that was one thing which I could never resist.

It wasn't worth trying to find the others, because I didn't know in which club or bar they'd arranged to meet. I was happy to be on my own, and it would make a change to go swimming by myself. As I walked slowly along the promenade, I wondered whether I dared to go swimming alone. I had no costume, and simply considering a solo moonlight swim made me feel vulnerable. Nude swimming with another person felt somehow safer.

But what did I have to fear? It certainly wasn't the ocean, or what it contained. The only thing to worry about was the land creatures – people. What bothered me, I realized, was that I might be seen. But so what? After some of the things I'd done on the beach, a stranger seeing me naked in the dark was nothing. I knew how close you had to be to even tell that someone was nude, let alone what sex they were.

I decided I'd do it: go for a midnight swim, alone and nude. I kept walking along the seafront, to where I was less likely to be seen. Reaching one of the flights of steps which was far enough away from the town centre, I walked down, removed my shoes, and started heading towards the ocean.

It was very quiet on the beach, as if the tranquillity of the sea absorbed all the noise from the town. The water was calm, with a gentle swell, and the only sound that could be heard was the soft lapping of the waves.

I walked down by one of the breakwaters, gazing around amongst the shadows for a darker shape which would show there was someone else nearby. Sometimes there were fishermen, but they always had lights. There was not a sound, not a movement, and I began to undress. I was stripped to the waist, the cool night breeze causing my nipples to harden, and about to remove my skirt when I thought I heard something. I became still, looking around and listening.

Sounds always seemed to travel further over the empty beach, the uncertain boundary where the land met the sea, and at night any noise was echoed and magnified across the ever-shifting frontier.

Then I realized I had not heard something – instead I'd *sensed* it. I was aware that I wasn't alone. Not too far away, perhaps on the next beach, maybe the one beyond that, there were other people. That should have made no difference to me. All I had to do was keep undressing and go down for a swim. If they saw me, so what?

Instead, I slipped my blouse back on, picked up my shoes and walked towards the next beach. Perhaps part of me already knew what I would discover, and that was what drew me to the other beach.

They were on the far side of the second breakwater, quite a distance away from where I halted, and if I hadn't known who they were I probably wouldn't have recognized the dim naked shapes. It was almost like a re-enactment of last week, I realized, except that Helen was playing my role.

I was on the other side of the breakwater, standing on tiptoe to see over the top as I peered through the darkness, trying to work out exactly what Helen was doing.

Once I realized, it was obvious: she was being fucked!

I stared, fascinated, then lowered my head and slowly moved closer. Every few seconds I halted, making sure that they were unaware of my presence. There was no danger of that, they were far too involved with what they were doing.

Helen was flat on her back, her legs outstretched. Danny was above her, his pale ass jerking up and down as he thrust his cock deep inside the girl. Simon was sitting nearby, watching.

Closer and closer I went, until I was exactly opposite them. I dared not move, dared not raise my head above the breakwater. The ancient wood was worn smooth by years of tidal activity, and I peered through a crack between the planks. I could see very little, but my imagination knew no limits. My heart was beating so fast I thought that I would be heard. But Helen was making far more noise, sighing and gasping and moaning and whimpering. As if in empathy, my own breath was coming in shorter and shorter bursts.

My best friend was fucking, being fucked, so close to me that I could have touched her if it weren't for the breakwater between us. Helen was fuck, fuck, fucking, being fuck, fuck, fucked . . .

This was for real.

And I was absolutely thrilled.

I wondered what would happen if I simply said 'hello' and climbed over the breakwater.

But I liked the idea of spying on Helen, of watching her being screwed without her knowing. Maybe I wasn't only an exhibitionist – I was also a voyeur. There was no reason why I couldn't be both.

I realized that I was fondling my breasts, and I watched as my right hand raised the hem of my skirt and slipped down into my panties. It was almost as if it were moving of its own volition. My fingers slid across my pubic hairs, down onto my labia. The lips were swollen and wet. My fingertips touched my clitoris, and I shivered with inner heat. I gently rolled my growing clit between thumb and index finger.

Simply thinking about what was happening was exciting me so much, but now I also wanted to see properly. I needed the extra stimulation of real fucking to take me higher than the fantasy image of Danny's prick sliding quickly in and out of Helen's twat.

I began to stand up. My fingers were still frantically working on my cunt, moving in the same primeval rhythm as the fucking sounds a few feet away. Helen's breathing was as fast as my own, but I tried not to cry out as I masturbated myself towards orgasm.

I looked over the breakwater, looked down at Helen.

'Ah, ah, ah, ah!' she moaned.

She looked up at me.

'Hi!' she added.

'Uh!' I said, sucking in air. Another stroke or two and I would ascend the highest of peaks.

Helen was still on her back, still being fucked, her arms curled around Danny's neck, her legs wrapped around his waist.

Except it wasn't Danny. Danny was the one sitting on the beach. It was –

'Simon!' I yelled.

It was the first and only time I called out his name as I climaxed, and it was as much a shout of anger as it was of triumphal delight.

Simon froze. He turned his head slightly, staring up at me.

'Ah-don't-ah-stop-ah!' Helen commanded, urging him to keep driving into her.

Danny beckoned to me. 'Come and join us,' he said.

'No, thank you,' I replied, very primly, as if declining an invitation to afternoon tea.

I only hoped that he couldn't guess that I was half-naked, my hand still inside my panties.

He shrugged and turned his attention back to Simon and Helen, who were still busy screwing.

I don't know what I expected, whether I assumed that they would suddenly stop at my command. I should have known that there was no way they could be separated, not at the height of passion. The image of a bucket of water being hurled over them came to mind. Although there was plenty of water nearby, there was no bucket.

I felt both angry and betrayed. How long had this been going on for? Surely it couldn't be the first occasion Simon had fucked Helen.

Then I glanced at Danny again. At first I'd thought he had been the one screwing her – and he had, I realized. While I'd been creeping up on the other side of the breakwater, he and Simon had swapped places. First Danny had been fucking Helen. Once he'd shot his load into her twat, it was Simon's turn to shaft her.

'*Ah-ah-ah-ah-ah-ah*-AH-AH-AH-AH-AH-AH-*AH-AH-AH-AH-AH-AH!!!*'

And all the time it had been Helen's turn.

Maybe that was it: I was jealous of her.

Tonight there were two hard cocks for Helen, two guys to fuck her, and I'd had nothing.

(My fingers were wet as I withdrew my hand, a reminder that tonight I'd certainly had more than nothing – but this was not a matter for logic.)

I was still standing in the same place, still watching as Simon's backside gave one final buck, and his whole body became totally rigid for a few seconds. I recognized the way that he froze when he ejaculated.

Perhaps it was my own fault. I should have let him fuck me. That was what he wanted. If I had, then he wouldn't have been shafting Helen.

At the same time as this thought occurred to me, I knew that it was wrong. Even if Simon had fucked me, he'd still have fucked Helen if given the opportunity. Whatever I did, it would have made no difference. It had very little to do with me.

In fact, all of this had very little to do with me.

In a few brief minutes, I'd experienced a whole spectrum of emotions and conflicting experiences. I'd been amazed and thrilled, surprised and stimulated; but I'd been shocked and disappointed, saddened and cheated.

Somewhere in the middle of all this, I'd had an orgasm.

Now I just felt confused, unsure what to do.

Helen and Simon were speaking to me, but I wasn't listening. I didn't want to hear. I didn't know what I did want.

'No,' I replied, to whatever it was they were saying. I kept shaking my head. 'No, no, no.'

I turned and headed back up the beach, away from the sea.

It wasn't until I got home that I realized I'd missed out on my swim.

What I did then was to fill the bath as full as possible, with water which was as hot as I could bear, and I lay soaking for ages. Because bathing took so long, first waiting for the bath to fill up, then getting the temperature right, I preferred taking a shower in order to get clean. Apart from washing, there had never seemed much to do in the bath. I'd occasionally tried reading, but the steam tended to make the pages damp, and I always liked to take care of my books.

Baths were good for thinking, however; not for any kind of constructive thoughts, but for allowing the mind to wander while the body relaxed. My mind kept wandering to one particular thing, one particular event. I tried to avoid the subject, but it seemed impossible.

I thought about Helen. Helen and Simon. Helen and Danny. Helen and Danny and Simon.

Then I thought about myself last week – me and Danny and Simon.

And I thought about fucking, about being fucked.

Helen had done it. She no longer had to wonder what it would be like, when it would first happen, who it would be with. I'd already suspected this to be the case, but now it had been graphically confirmed.

Seeing Simon fucking her had been a great surprise, although I should have guessed. But having crept up in order to spy on Helen, what did I expect? It had to be either Danny or Simon – it just happened to be both of them.

It didn't matter. What did I care? I'd certainly enjoyed myself at first, as I leaned against the break-water and listened to the sounds of frantic fucking, while beginning to masturbate.

As I remembered, I smiled, and I realized that both of my hands were resting on my crotch. My legs parted slightly, my right hand slipped between my thighs, my index and third finger pressed against my labia, gently massaging the swollen flesh, while the tip of my middle finger glided across my clitoris before sliding even further down – and further in than ever before.

That was when I discovered there was something else that I could do in the bath . . .

Although it was my day off, I woke up at the usual time. Because I didn't have to get up early, I remained in bed, finally drifting off to sleep once more.

When I woke up again, it was two hours later. Something had made me wake, and I wondered what it could have been. A knock on the front door? I stayed where I was, cosy and curled up.

While I was at work, I was forced to stay indoors; but now I had the opportunity of being outside, I didn't take it. The difference was that the choice was mine. I'd get up when I was ready, go outside when I was ready – if I wanted to.

I only had another week of work, after which it was back to school. That always seemed to be the end of summer, although I knew it wasn't true. We usually had long spells of good weather before the holidays, and there were frequent periods of good weather afterwards. Sometimes I thought the worst weather of all was during the height of the season.

Having hardly spent any of the holidays on the beach, I'd probably go there today, make the most of it while I could.

It was only then that I remembered I'd been on the beach the previous night. So had Danny and Simon and Helen . . .

The telephone started to ring downstairs. That was what must have woken me a minute ago, I realized. I lay where I was, letting it ring. If it was for my parents, they were out. If it was for me, it would be Helen or Simon or maybe even Danny, still hoping to ask me out. I lay absolutely still, as if whoever was phoning would have known that I was in the house if I moved; they could have sensed me over the telephone wires, known that I was refusing to answer.

I waited until it had stopped ringing before I got up, then peered through the bedroom curtains, confirming what a beautiful day it was. The sky was pale blue, with only a few small clouds in the distance. It was too good a day to waste indoors.

'The beach for you,' I told my naked image in the mirror. I remembered that I'd missed out on my swim yesterday. 'But you'll have to wear your swimsuit. That'll make a change.'

I found a long T-shirt, one I often wore in bed, and pulled it on. It hung to just below my buttocks – unless I bent over or stretched upwards. I remembered that as I yawned and stretched out my arms, and the hem of the T-shirt rode up above my pubic hairs.

I went downstairs to the kitchen, opened the back door to allow in some fresh air, and wondered if I was hungry enough to make myself some breakfast. As I went back into the hall to find a magazine to flick through while I decided, the telephone rang. Automatically, I picked it up.

'Wrong number,' I said.

'Are you still mad at me?' It was Helen.

'For fucking my boyfriend, why should I be mad?'

I realized I'd said 'boyfriend'. Did I really think that was what Simon was? I must have done, and I didn't like the idea. No, he definitely wasn't my 'boyfriend'. He was nothing to me. He could fuck whoever he wanted. Helen could fuck him if she liked – but I wasn't going to tell her that . . .

'Just a wild guess,' said Helen.

I said nothing, waiting for her to continue.

'Are you still there?'

'No,' I said.

'If you're waiting for me to apologize, to say I'm sorry, then I'll say it: "I'm sorry".'

'You're lying.'

'Yes,' agreed Helen, and she laughed.

I smiled, but again I said nothing.

'If you hadn't stayed at work, it wouldn't have happened.'

'Oh, I see,' I said, 'then it's all my fault?'

'That's right. Isn't it always? It just happened, you know.'

'I don't know.'

'They waved their magic wands and what could a poor, weak, helpless, defenceless, young, gorgeous, beautiful girl do?'

'I've no idea. But I know what you did.'

Helen laughed again, and I almost did.

'We've been friends a long time, haven't we?' she said. 'We're not going to let something like this come between us, are we?'

'Something so small, you mean?'

'Exactly! And why are penises so small?'

'Why?'

'Because that's where guys keep their brains.'

'And which of them has the most brains?' I asked.

It was a risky question. I already knew that Danny's cock was bigger than Simon's, because I'd handled the evidence. But did Helen know what had happened the previous week? Had one of the boys told her, and that was why she tried to go further than I had done?

'They're all the same in the dark,' Helen replied.

And this time I couldn't hide my laughter.

'What are you doing today?' she asked.

'Nothing – and lots of it.'

'Why don't you come around here and do that?'

'You're not working at your parents' place?'

'I knew that you had the day off, so I thought I'd take the day off. How about it? You want to come around? You haven't been here this summer, have you?'

I was very tempted, although I didn't want to give in too easily.

I said: 'Well . . . '

During previous years, Helen and I used to spend many days in her garden. It was large and secluded, a perfect sun trap. We would do nothing except talk, tan – and drink wine. The first time I'd ever been drunk had been in Helen's garden. Also the second, third, fourth time . . .

'There's plenty to drink,' said Helen.

'What else have you got to offer?'

'I could make lunch.'

'Well . . . ' I could still remember Helen's idea of cooking.

'No, no. Because of the restaurant, I'm getting good at lunches.'

'I wanted to go for a swim.'

'We could do that as well.'

'At midnight?'

'Perhaps a bit before that. How about it?'

I sighed theatrically. 'I suppose so.'

'Try and curb your enthusiasm. I'll start pouring the wine. See you in a few minutes.'

'Just one thing.'

'What?'

74

'Two things, I mean.'

'What? What?'

'We don't talk about Simon or Danny.'

'Okay.'

The problem of breakfast seemed to be solved: it would be wine.

I made my way back upstairs to get ready and collect my things. I didn't need much. A swimsuit for swimming, but a bikini for sunbathing. I wore as little as possible when it was hot, and I dressed quickly: skimpy T-shirt, pair of shorts, sandals.

The phone rang again.

'But can we talk about their cocks?'

'No!' I replied, and hung up.

Chapter Six

'Hi,' said Helen.

She was half-naked. The top half. She'd opened the front door wearing only a pair of very abbreviated yellow bikini pants, and stood there in full view of anyone going by.

I simply stared in amazement. I'd seen her totally naked, of course, but only at night. To see her like this during the day was a great surprise.

'Er . . . hi,' I said, raising my eyes from her boobs and hoping I hadn't stared for too long.

'Come in.'

I went into the hall, and Helen closed the door and led the way through to the kitchen. That was when I noticed her bare behind.

Her bikini pants were new, or new to me. At the front there was little more than a triangle of flimsy fabric which barely covered her pubis. The rest of the garment was made up of very slender ribbons, the horizontal one tucked up within the crease of her behind. Her buttocks were completely exposed. Perhaps it wasn't the lower half of a bikini, but the whole outfit – a monokini.

Seeing Helen like this was nothing compared to what I'd seen her doing last night, I supposed. Then I realized that I hadn't actually *seen* very much the previous night. Although I knew what she had been doing, I hadn't been able to observe very much detail. Simon had been fucking her, but also obscuring the view, so there hadn't been much to see: no length of prick sliding in and out of her cunt. In fact, Helen had seen far more of me the night she'd watched me wanking Simon, when his spunk had spurted all over my body and I'd then used it as lubricant to masturbate myself.

What I'd done made Helen's bare boobs seem very modest – although I still wondered what she was up to. There was no way I could avoid looking at her breasts. Her nipples were much darker than mine.

'Red or white?' asked Helen.

I couldn't pretend that nothing odd was happening, and so I gave up my own pretence and studied her impressive boobs.

'White,' I said, 'but they'll probably go red in the sun.'

Helen glanced at her tits, and she smiled. 'The wine, I mean.'

'Whatever you're having.'

So she opened a bottle of red, a bottle of white, poured two glasses of each. While she did this, my eyes were on her breasts, watching the way they jiggled as she moved, how they rose and fell as she stretched or bent down. When Helen had opened the door, her dark nipples had been totally smooth. By now they were erect. So were my own, pressing hard against the fabric of my T-shirt.

I couldn't believe that I was getting turned on by another girl's sleek bare flesh, and I tried to change the focus of my attention, thinking of algebraic formulae. That didn't succeed, so I went on to trigonometry. Then I abandoned mathematics, because I was still on holiday, and I reached for a glass of white wine. I swallowed half in one gulp.

'Shall we go into the garden?' said Helen, taking a glass in each hand.

'Yeah.' I followed her out, my eyes focusing on her buttocks as she walked onto the sunlit patio. I carried the rest of my glass of wine in one hand, my bag in the other. I glanced around the garden, checking the trees and the fences which masked it from view.

'No one can see us,' said Helen. 'Or I wouldn't be dressed like this.'

'Really?' I said. 'Don't you mean *undressed*? And what about when you came to the front door?'

I remembered when I first got up that morning, I'd carefully peeped between my bedroom curtains. That was because I was nude – and there was a one in a thousand chance someone might have been staring up at the window.

'That was just to surprise you,' Helen answered.

'You did. But what if it wasn't me at the door? It could have been the postman.'

'Pity it wasn't. He's a real hunk. He could shove whatever he wants into my box any time!' Her eyes widened at the thought, and she grinned.

This was no longer an idle remark, I supposed – not after last night.

'What's the idea, anyway?' I asked, as I sat down on one of the two sun loungers.

'What idea?'

In reply, I gazed at her bare boobs again.

'I thought I'd get more of a tan,' Helen answered.

This wasn't the first time she'd sunned herself like this, I noticed. Her complexion was darker than mine, but I'd realized that she was also tanned – and her breasts were the same colour as the rest of her skin.

'But I wouldn't do this on the beach,' she continued, 'not like all those foreign girls.'

'What foreign girls?'

'The students, you know. They all lie topless near the pier.'

'I haven't noticed. It's the boys I look at. I'm not a lesbian.'

Helen laughed at our old joke, and I smiled.

'You must have seen them,' she insisted.

'No.' I shook my head. 'I've hardly been down to the beach this summer.' I paused. 'At least, not during the day . . . ' I sipped my wine, remembering.

Helen took two sips, one from each glass. 'There's been quite a fuss. Letters and news reports in the local paper about it – with photos to prove how disgusting it is.'

'But they lie on their fronts, don't they?'

'Their backs,' Helen said. 'Tits upwards.'

'Oh.'

'Would you do it?'

'Be half-naked on the beach? Never! Not during the day. Completely nude in the middle of the night, maybe . . . !'

We both laughed. I watched as Helen's bare breasts bounced up and down, and she watched me. I knew what she was waiting for – for me to undress.

'I know it happens abroad a lot,' I said, trying to continue the conversation – any conversation. 'Girls going topless.'

'It happens here now. In this country. In this town.'

'And there are lots of nudist beaches abroad.'

'There are here. In this country – although not in this town.'

'I can't see why anyone should mind. You see bare boobs in the newspapers, on television, in films. What's the difference if it's' – I shrugged – 'in the flesh?'

I wondered whether I was trying to convince myself or not. I'd been naked with Helen before, but it had always been at night, when different rules seemed to apply. The first time we'd stripped off together had been to go for a swim, and there seemed no such excuse now. It didn't seem right to peel off my T-shirt without any justification. Then I reasoned that having no excuse was a good enough excuse.

I stretched my arms wide, and my breasts became moulded against the fabric of my T-shirt, the nipples clearly outlined. Helen watched, saying nothing, as I took another slow sip of wine. Then I casually raised my T-shirt, up over my bare breasts, then over my head. Helen looked at my tits and nodded her approval. She raised one of her wine glasses in a toast. I lifted my own glass in salute.

Having equalled Helen's state of semi-nudity, I felt more relaxed. But that only lasted for a few seconds, until I realized I had to worry about getting out of my shorts and into my bikini pants.

I could just keep them on, but that would seem odd, and I wondered how I should proceed to discard them. There was no way I could simply take them off in front of Helen, because that would mean being completely nude. And to do that in full daylight was far too extreme. Perhaps I could turn my back on her, so that only my bum was visible while I changed. But if I did that, she'd know that I was too embarrassed to let her see me fully naked. After everything we had been through together, it would appear very strange if I went into the house only to return a few seconds later wearing even less.

At the same time, all of this seemed an impossible dilemma. If only I'd known how easy it was to undress in front of other people. It's the simplest thing in the world, and it doesn't matter if one person is watching or a hundred. It doesn't matter whether that one person is a man or a woman, and it doesn't matter if a whole crowd is staring at your nude body – in fact, it's great to be the centre of so much attention. And the best way to become the focus of attention is by being naked.

'I suppose it's because they're away from home,' said Helen.

'Who?'

'The foreign students. They're away from home. No one knows them. They can do whatever they want. Being topless on the beach is the least of what they get up to while they're here. They go wild, completely cock-crazy.'

I glanced at Helen, thinking it wasn't only the foreign girls who behaved that way, but I said nothing.

'If this wasn't my home town,' continued Helen, 'I might go on the beach like this.'

'And let everyone see you?' I said.

'Isn't that the idea?'

'I thought the idea was to get a suntan.'

Helen shrugged, and her breasts swayed. I realized that I was being careful to keep mine from moving. Even when I'd peeled off my T-shirt, I'd done it very slowly, keeping my torso rigid.

'I don't mind people seeing me,' said Helen. 'Except people I know. Imagine meeting the head teacher on the beach, and him seeing your bare tits! He'd have a heart attack.'

'Maybe if he saw yours, he would.' And to prove I could match Helen's conversational level, I added: 'If he saw mine, he'd cream himself!'

At school, once a girl began to develop breasts she had to wear a bra. When I'd been younger, I couldn't wait to grow up and buy my first bra. Now, the only time I ever wore one was when I was at school.

I tilted my glass to my lips, draining the wine. I watched the subtle difference in the curve of my right breast as my arm was raised and lowered – and I noticed that Helen was also watching.

'Talking of cream, you could do with some on your tits.'

'I know I could!' I grinned and touched my fingertips to my breast, remembering it streaked with spunk.

'You know what I mean,' said Helen, who knew exactly what I meant. 'There's nothing as bad as burned nipples.'

'Having them chewed?' I suggested.

'Having them chewed is better.' As she spoke, she took her right nipple between finger and thumb, and I saw it respond, growing instantly larger at her touch.

81

Then her hand slid lower, cupping her breast, pushing it upwards, and she lowered her head.

I watched in total astonishment as her tongue flickered out, licking the nipple. Then her lips engulfed the firm flesh as she sucked it into her mouth.

She only tongued her tit for a second, but immediately my heart began to pound, my pulse began to race, and I felt drops of sweat appear on my warm flesh. I was suddenly very hot, and not because of the sun and the wine. The heat was radiating from one part of my body: my cunt.

Sucking my own nipples was something I had never considered, never even dreamed of doing. But as I gazed at Helen, that wasn't what I imagined.

Instead, I thought of sucking her nipples.

I thought of *me* sucking her nipples . . .

'It's not as good,' said Helen, raising her head from her saliva-soaked nipples. 'It's like tickling. You can't do it to yourself.' She gazed at me, then added: 'Not like . . .'

She raised her index finger, curling it. Then she grinned and suddenly jumped to her feet.

'I'll get some suntan cream.'

I watched her vanish into the house, and I breathed out slowly. For a few seconds I wondered if I ought to go home. What was she going to do next? But, I realized, I was enjoying myself. This was a different kind of sexual arousal that I was now feeling. I'd had sex with myself, sex with Simon and sex with Danny. Not 'sex' in its restricted sense, which was fucking. There was more to sex than that, far more.

The idea of sex with another girl was very stimulating, I discovered, because it seemed so forbidden. I wasn't thinking of any kind of physical contact between myself and Helen, and I very much doubted that it could ever come to that. We had been best friends far too long to become lovers. I wasn't even sure what women *did* to each other, how they became lovers – but whatever it was, I was sure I couldn't do it to Helen and she couldn't do it to me.

Then I remembered my thought about sucking her nipple . . .

Which was probably how sex would start between two women.

But that was only a fantasy, I knew. Helen and I would simply spend a few hours together, talking and laughing and drinking, the way we always had. Maybe we would be half-naked. So what? And maybe what we talked about and did would arouse each other. So what? There was nothing serious going on. I already knew that Helen had only licked her tit to try and shock me.

We had both discovered sex very recently, and it was only natural that we were totally fascinated by the subject. We had always talked easily together. And that's all we would do: talk. We could be as daring as we wanted with each other. There was no danger in this kind of sex, without the male of the species.

Helen had only been teasing me so far, and I'd played along. If one of us were male, however, it wouldn't be long until we went beyond that stage of the game.

I touched my left nipple with the side of my wine glass, and it grew harder. There were still a few drops of wine at the bottom of the glass. I raised the glass towards my lips, then hesitated. I tilted the glass, and the chilled drops fell onto my nipple, and I sighed with pleasure at the sensation. As I gazed down, I imagined that it was Helen's breast. I started to lower my head, as if I were going to lick the sweet liquid from her tender flesh.

Then I heard a sound from inside the house, and I glanced up quickly, thinking that Helen was coming out; but there was no sign of her. The moment was lost, and I stood up. While she was gone, I had the chance of changing without her seeing me.

I quickly thumbed down my shorts and stepped out of them. I still had my sandals on, which slowed me down because one leg of my shorts became entangled. Then I cast them aside and opened my bag. There was so much stuff inside that at first I couldn't find my bikini. Then I saw the red fabric, and I pulled. But it was only the bra, which I discarded as I rummaged deeper into my bag. Finally, I found my briefs, and I started to pull them on. First my right leg, then the left. But my sandal strap became caught again. I stood on one leg, trying to free my briefs.

That was when I heard another sound, the noise of someone tapping on a window. I looked around and saw Helen. She was watching me from the back room, her breasts flattened where they were pressed up against the glass. She smiled and waved.

It didn't bother me that Helen had been watching, not considering everything else she had seen. I was half tempted to remain naked. Instead, I undid the sandal, kicked it away, pulled up my red briefs, unfastened the other sandal, then headed into the kitchen for my other glass of wine. Helen came through, carrying a bottle of suntan oil in one hand and a glossy magazine in the other. She glanced down at my now-covered crotch, and again she smiled.

'You know what I've always envied of yours?' she said.

'My brains, my beauty, or both?'

'Your hair.'

'This?' I said, running my fingers through my scalp.

'And that.' She nodded down to my crotch.

'You've never seen that before. Not in daylight, anyway.'

'I've seen enough.'

I glanced down, not understanding what she meant. The next thing I saw was Helen's hand reaching towards my briefs. I was so amazed that I did nothing even when her fingers touched the edge of the fabric.

She pinched a wisp of my pubic hair between thumb and forefinger, and she pulled.

'It's such a wonderful colour, you don't even notice when it strays from your knickers,' she said. She let go, allowing the pubic curl to spring back. 'But whenever we've tried on clothes together, I've noticed.' She shook her head. 'You're so lucky.' Then she turned and headed out into the sunshine.

I remained frozen, totally amazed by the casually intimate way that Helen had tugged at my pubes. After a few seconds, I drained my glass of red wine. I picked up one of the bottles and filled the glass again. More wine seemed to go onto the table than into my glass, because my hands were shaking. I felt very calm within, however, maybe because of the alcohol I'd already consumed. My senses felt more alert than ever.

Helen, I realized, was carrying the game to an even higher level. But I wouldn't let her beat me. I leaned down to sip my full glass, not wanting to lose any more, then followed her outside.

'Even when we were kids,' Helen continued, 'I wished that my hair was like yours. I love the way it becomes so golden in the summer. You ought to grow it longer, as long as possible. Then you could go topless on the beach and still keep your tits covered.' She smiled at the idea. 'Imagine having long blonde hair, with the nipples almost peeping through, so anyone watching isn't sure if they can see them or not.'

'You could grow your hair,' I said, as I sat down.

'I have done. And what happens?'

She pulled at one of her thick, jet black locks, tugging it down below her breasts. As soon as she let go, it coiled back upwards.

'And you don't even have to shave your legs,' she added, running her hands over her calves. 'Your hairs are almost invisible.'

I nodded. My hair was very fine, very pale, but

because I was used to it this was something I'd never really considered before. Helen's legs were hairless, but only because they had been depilated. I'd never done that, never had to remove a single hair from my body – not even under my arms. All I'd ever grown were a few soft wisps which hardly seemed worth bothering about. They were part of me, the way I was, so why should I get rid of them?

'I think some of them were visible a few minutes ago,' I said, looking Helen in the eye. And this time it was my turn to reach down to my crotch and tug at a frond of blonde curls, unwinding the strand and pulling it as far out as it would go. I was surprised how long it was.

'My pubes are a bit darker than the hair on my hair,' I said. 'They don't get bleached by the light.'

'Darker?' said Helen. 'You don't know the meaning of the word. You want to see dark?'

And she pulled out one of her own pubic curls. It was as black as the hair on her head – as black as I'd guessed from having seen her on the beach at night.

Until now I hadn't paid any attention to Helen's pubic hairs; but I realized that she never had stray hairs curling out from her panties, and that at night her dark triangle had seemed smaller than mine. Even the length of hair she now stretched out from beneath her monokini couldn't match the one I'd unravelled.

Her other arm was bent behind her neck, displaying her hairless armpit, and from what she said her legs had been similarly shaven. That was when I realized: Helen must also have cropped her pubic hairs. It was no different from cutting her fingernails, I supposed. If something grew too long, she trimmed it.

'It's as if it has nothing to do with my body,' Helen added, as she continued twisting the tuft of hair around her fingers. 'It's like a black arrow pointing at my cunt.' She shook her head. 'What's it for? Why do we need to have hair down there?'

I shrugged. 'To keep us warm?'

'I've never had a cold twat. I know perfectly well how to keep it warm.' She raised her index finger, and there was no need for her to curl it for me to know what she meant.

'Perhaps,' I suggested, 'when we lived in caves they hadn't invented masturbation.'

'Which came first, the wheel or wanking?'

'History would be a lot more interesting if we studied that,' I said.

'The origins of finger-fucking, for example,' said Helen. She was still coiling black pubic hairs around her finger, except her finger slowly started to slide beneath the yellow fabric of her monokini. She glanced up at me, sighed, then withdrew her hand with a mock reluctance which was probably only partly feigned.

'If I had hair like yours,' she continued, 'I wouldn't just go topless – I'd go nude.'

'Like this?' I said.

It was time for me to go further than her. So I raised my hips from the chair and thumbed down my bikini pants, slid them over my thighs, down my legs, off my ankles, and kicked them away.

I leaned back, absolutely naked, and drank some more wine.

At last I felt totally free. It was like being nude on the beach for the first time. I was outside, it was very hot, so why should I bother wearing anything? There was no one else to see me except Helen – and even if there were, I didn't care.

'This is the life,' I said.

'Yes,' agreed Helen, as she peeled off her flimsy pants, 'it is.'

We looked at each other.

'See what I mean?' she said, plucking at her pubic hairs.

I shrugged. It was true that the contrast between

the black triangle and her pale skin did draw my eyes towards her twat – but my eyes would have been directed there in any case.

Helen shook her head, drank some more wine, then glanced up at the sun. Our chairs had been opposite one another, but now she moved her own so that they were side by side, both facing the sun. She picked up the suntan oil and offered it to me.

'Thanks,' I said, reaching across.

She drew her hand back a fraction. 'You want me to rub it in for you?' she asked, mischievously, her eyes on my breasts.

'Okay,' I said, deciding to call her bluff.

'You'd let me, wouldn't you?' she laughed, and she passed me the bottle.

And I realized that I would have done. Instead, I massaged the oil into my own flesh, paying special attention to the areas which had never previously been exposed to sunlight. I rubbed my breasts until they gleamed. The oil gave my dilated nipples a glittering shine, as if their pinkness were a reflection of the sun.

'Any excuse to touch yourself up,' Helen remarked, as she picked up the magazine she had brought out. Her nipples were as firm as mine, I noticed.

'Who needs an excuse?' I asked, closing my eyes.

My oily hands slid down my torso and began smearing the liquid over my stomach and towards my hips. I gradually circled my pudenda, until every millimetre of flesh was coated right up to the edge of my pubic hairs. When masturbating, I'd never used anything as lubricant apart from water while in the shower or bath, or my own spit when in bed – except for the time I'd used Simon's silvery spunk. But I liked the texture of the suntan oil, and if I'd been alone my fingers would probably have ventured even further, even deeper.

I felt totally relaxed, totally calm. I was warm, content – and, after three glasses of wine, quite drunk. Having finished oiling myself, I held out the bottle for

Helen, but she didn't take it. When I opened my eyes, I noticed she was flicking through the magazine.

'What's that?' I asked, dreamily, thinking it was some fashion mag.

'Take a look,' she said, throwing it onto my lap as she stood up. 'You want some more wine?'

'No thanks.'

'What?'

'Well, okay. A small glass. One small glass.'

I watched as she headed into the kitchen, admiring her trim waist, the way that her hips swayed from side to side, and how her firm buttocks rocked up and down. She must have sensed my eyes on her, because she turned around as she reached the door. I didn't know why she was complaining about her pubic hairs, they contrasted perfectly with her soft pale flesh. Just as Helen claimed to envy my hair, I'd always liked hers. It was so thick and curly that it always looked good, even if she hadn't washed it for several days. Some days she didn't even bother combing or brushing her hair, but it still looked great.

I picked up the magazine and began turning the pages, not really paying much attention at first. But it didn't take long until I was totally riveted. It wasn't a fashion magazine. The models weren't wearing any of the latest designs.

In fact, they weren't wearing anything.

I was holding what was known as a men's magazine. It was the first time I'd ever opened one. I'd seen them for sale, and I knew what they contained. They were full of photos of naked women.

And I was almost right.

But there was far more to it than that.

Instead of just glamorous nude pictures of bare-breasted beauties, as totally naked as Helen and I were, the illustrations were far more explicit.

There were pages and pages of glossy nudes, but the emphasis wasn't on their tits or buttocks. The central focus for most of the photos was on one certain part of the female anatomy. If I'd ever considered the matter, that was probably what I'd have expected. The magazine was aimed at men, and the part of a woman which interested men the most was what they didn't have themselves: the cunt.

Most of the models were in such strange poses, lying with their legs spread, or bending over, or twisting around – and the only reason for this was to make sure that their wet twats were opened wide for the camera. Many of the photographs were in such close-up that the girls' vaginas were life-size, and every intimate detail was revealed in full colour.

All I could do was stare in astonishment. The pictures didn't excite me. They were only photos of girls, of their cunts.

But I'd never even seen my own vulva in such detail. If I'd ever thought to examine myself with a mirror, I could have studied my inner and outer labia, but the idea had never occurred to me. And I knew my clitoris only by touch, although sometimes I'd glanced down while masturbating and seen the pink bud glistening between my golden cunt curls.

As I turned the pages, I studied the girls' faces instead of their twats. I gazed deep into their eyes and wondered why they were so willing to expose blatantly the rosy heart of their femininity.

But, as the saying goes, little did I know . . .

Chapter Seven

'What *are* you doing?' asked Helen.

I glanced up from the picture of the nude girl lying on a four-poster bed to the nude girl who was coming from the kitchen, a brimming glass of wine in each hand. The girl in the photograph had her left leg bent out at the hip, while her right leg was thrust up in the air, supported by her right hand. Without realizing, I had been trying to copy her position.

I let my right leg fall back onto the sun lounger, pressing my left one up against it. I hoped that Helen hadn't seen as much of my cunt as I'd seen of the girl's in the magazine. There was a great difference between showing my pubic hairs and spreading my legs to expose my labia.

'Where did you get this from?' I asked.

'I thought you didn't want to talk about that subject.'

I presumed she meant it was Danny's magazine.

'That's why some of the pages might be stuck together,' she added.

I frowned. 'Why?'

Helen made a loose fist of her right hand, jerked it up and down, and I nodded in understanding. If I'd thought about it enough, I'd have guessed what such magazines were really for.

'Interesting, isn't it?' said Helen, putting one of the glasses of wine next to me.

'Very educational,' I replied, as I turned to the next page. It was the same girl in another pose, and I twisted the magazine around, then upside down, wondering how she had managed to get herself into such contortions. It looked as though she was trying to turn herself inside out, and all so that her cunt lips were spread as wide as possible. It would have taken another glass or two of wine before I'd have attempted to imitate that pose.

'I borrowed it without him knowing,' Helen added, as she sat down next to me, 'and I haven't really looked at it yet.'

I kept turning the pages. The boobs and bums and twats didn't turn me on, although somehow I was hypnotized by all the images of sleek naked female flesh. There was more to the magazine than pictures of nude girls – although not much. I supposed that the various articles and features and letters were there simply to pad out the publication. Without them, a collection of pictures of unclad females would soon become boring. If you'd seen one twat, you'd seen them all.

Or maybe I only thought that because I was female. If I were male, I supposed, then there could be no such thing as too much. I knew enough of the opposite sex to realize that whatever they had, they always wanted more. Even when they were out on a date, guys always looked at other girls.

But as I flicked through the magazine, I realized that there were differences in the pictures. There were different girls, of course, and they were in different poses, in various different states of undress, and viewed in different locations: which meant different bedrooms, although sometimes they were naked in a different room. To me, there didn't seem enough variety – although I supposed that the subject didn't really allow for that.

Then I reached the centre of the magazine, and instead of one naked girl there were two. The sequence of photos was almost like a story, although there wasn't much of a plot. It started with the two girls being fully dressed, showed them peeling off each other's glamorous clothes, stripping down to their exotic underwear. Then their undies came off, until finally they were completely nude – both with their legs wide open, one of them lying on top of the other, each with her wet tongue probing towards the other's gaping twat. Both tongues and both twats were visible because of the huge mirror which was positioned behind them.

'That's a good idea,' said Helen, as she stared at the photo of the two girls. She sipped at her wine, then leaned closer for a better view.

'I am not,' I said slowly, 'going to lick your clit.'

Helen glanced at me. She looked puzzled for a moment, but then she nodded and glanced at the illustration again.

'Why not?' she asked. 'I can't lick my own, so . . .' She could go no further, because she suddenly started laughing. 'You know the saying: *You scratch my back, I'll scratch yours.* Well . . .'

'There's a lot of difference between that,' I said, gesturing towards the picture, 'and scratching.'

'Not much. They both get rid of an itch, don't they?'

'What's it called?'

'What?'

'You know – oral sex. Cunty-something.'

'Cunnilingus,' said Helen. 'But I didn't mean that was a good idea, although if you want to try . . .'

She ducked as I swiped at her with the magazine.

'Open it again at that page,' she told me, and I did. 'See the one reflected in the mirror? The one with her bum in the air. Look at her cunt.'

I could hardly avoid looking, but I still didn't understand why Helen was so interested.

'Here.' Helen took the magazine from me and turned to the previous page, where the girls were removing each other's frilly black lingerie. She tapped her finger against one of the two models. 'There.'

I suddenly noticed what Helen meant. The girl's

pudenda was completely smooth, without a single pubic hair.

'*That*'s a good idea,' Helen repeated. 'That's what I should do.' She ran the fingers of her free hand through her jet black curls. 'Shave them off.'

I laughed, thinking she was joking. She looked at me, and I realized that she was half-serious.

'What for?' I asked.

'So they don't stick out from my swimsuit. As I said before, if my hair was the same colour as yours it wouldn't matter.' She tugged at her pubes. 'But I don't need them and I don't want them. I already trim my pubic hairs, so why not shave them off? It's only like doing my legs. Men shave their beards, so what's the difference?'

It sounded as though she was trying to convince herself.

'Have you ever kissed a guy with a beard?' she asked, suddenly, and when I shook my head, she added: 'I wonder if it's any different.'

I pointed towards the magazine. 'Different like that, you mean?'

Helen looked at the two girls who were about to kiss each other's cunt. 'Imagine getting all those hairs in your mouth,' she said. She pulled a face, and mimed pulling hairs from her tongue.

She kept staring at the picture, and she thrust her tongue out even further, curling it upwards. She was holding the magazine in her left hand, and her right hand was still toying with her pubic hairs.

'You aren't going to use wax, are you?' I said.

Helen winced at the idea. She let the magazine fall, both of her hands dropping defensively over her crotch.

'Can you imagine it?' she said, and she shuddered.

I tried not to imagine smearing wax over my pubis, tried not to imagine sticking a piece of fabric to the wax, tried not to imagine ripping off the fabric, tried not to imagine all my pubic hairs being torn out by the roots . . .

I realized that my own hands were also protectively cradling my pubic mound.

'I think I'll use scissors,' said Helen, as she ran her fingers through her black triangle.

I looked at her, and she seemed more serious than before, although I knew that with Helen appearances could be very deceptive. This could be just another joke, all a part of the game.

'Just because it grows there doesn't mean I have to keep it,' she said. 'It's like body odour, something to be got rid of. A girl's got to make the most of her appearance.'

I wasn't really listening; Helen was talking for her own benefit, not mine. I tugged at one of my pubic curls, stretching it out, then I pulled at another. They were long enough to tie into a bow, but they kept springing free. And I realized how drunk I must have been.

'I've got plenty of ribbons if you want,' said Helen. 'What colour would you prefer?'

I tried to imagine what I'd look like with ribbons in my pubes, and I laughed and shook my head.

Helen drained her wine glass and stood up. She went inside, and I picked up the magazine again. I tried to read some of the captions under the photographs, but my eyes couldn't seem to focus on the words. I let the magazine slide to the ground and I lay back in the chair, gazing up into the clear blue sky.

Lying naked on a hot summer day, a glass of wine by my side, it was almost paradise. I only wished that I could have been right by the sea.

I heard a sound, and I looked around. Helen was back again. She was unravelling her pubic hairs with her left hand, stretching them out, and snipping them off with the pair of scissors in her right. That was when I knew for certain that she was absolutely serious.

'Are you sure about this?' I asked.

'Yes.' *Snip*.

'And it's just to get a tanned twat?'

'No!' *Snip*. 'It's for fun.' *Snip*. 'And don't make me laugh, this is a delicate operation.'

'You've given yourself a trim before?'

'Yes. I've run a comb through' – *snip* – 'and clipped off anything that's too long.'

'A comb?'

Snip. 'Yeah.' *Snip*. 'Don't you comb yours?' *Snip*.

I shook my head. I'd never even thought of combing my pubic hairs, let alone pruning them.

'Here.' Helen reached down to the make-up bag she'd brought out, and she passed me a small comb.

I took it, and tentatively ran the teeth through my fair curls. At first I thought it would soon get caught, that my untamed pubes must all be tangled and knotted, but the comb went through quite easily. The sensation of lightly tugging at my pubic hairs was very pleasant, I discovered. It was almost like having someone else stroking me.

Helen lay cutting her pubic hairs, while I lay combing mine. I glanced at her, and I laughed.

'What's so funny?' she asked.

'This is. What would anyone think if they saw us?'

She glanced at me, glanced down at herself, and she also laughed. 'That we're both perverts, I suppose.'

By now her legs were wide, and she was leaning forward, her head bent as close as possible as she started to clip between her thighs.

I winced. 'Be careful.' I bit my lip, not wanting to watch, but unable to look away.

After a couple of minutes, Helen leaned back, brushing away loose hairs with her fingers. She scratched at herself, then ran her fingertips across the bristles.

'A crew cut!' she announced.

'Is that it?' I asked.

'How's it look?' Helen stood up and turned towards

96

me, her crotch two feet from my face. Now that it was only covered by a short crop, her mound of venus was visible. I could even detect a trace of her labia.

'Er . . . '

'Bit of a mess, isn't it?' She frowned, and it seemed that she wished she'd never started. 'I can't get any closer with the scissors, but it's all got to go.'

'Tweezers?' I suggested.

'Ah . . . !' She shook her head at the thought. 'No, I'm going to have to shave it.'

'With a blade?'

'It can't be much different from doing my legs.'

'It can,' I said. 'It's . . . well . . . a more complicated shape.'

'What about an electric razor? I bet that would feel nice. Think of the vibration buzzing up and down.'

'That's probably better,' I agreed, although I wondered what Helen's father would think if he found out what she'd done with his electric shaver.

'But there isn't one in the house,' she said, as she found a long hair which had escaped the scissors. 'It'll have to be the razor.' *Snip*.

She reached down for her wine glass, draining it as she rubbed at her cropped pubis. Then she glanced back at me. I was still toying with my own pubic hairs, running the comb through them. They seemed to have become bushier, no longer pressed hard against my skin by my underwear.

'You?' asked Helen, and she offered me the scissors.

I shook my head quickly.

Helen continued searching for stray hairs, and finally she said: 'I suppose I'd better do it.'

She turned and went inside. I continued combing through my curls for a while, before putting the comb down. Then I thought that I ought to give it a wash before handing it back to Helen. If I'd been using it on my head I wouldn't have bothered, but after what I'd done it seemed only polite to wash the comb. I reached for my wine glass, but it was again empty. As I stood up, I almost lost my balance, and I realized that I shouldn't have any more to drink. Carefully, I picked up the comb, went into the house and headed for the bathroom.

I don't know what I was thinking. More likely, I wasn't thinking. Maybe I'd assumed that Helen was going to come out into the garden again to finish her depilation. Instead, she was sitting on the edge of the bath, spraying shaving foam over her crotch.

Her eyes were closed; she was smiling dreamily. She held the aerosol can in her left hand, her thumb on the button, and streaks of foam oozed out of the nozzle. It could almost have been spunk, except there was so much of it. The semen from a dozen cocks, I thought. And Helen's right hand was massaging the thick white bubbles between her legs. No wonder her eyes were shut, her expression so content.

I felt myself beginning to glow deep within. The pictures in the magazine had done nothing for me, but I was starting to become stimulated by watching Helen gently masturbate herself. I should have backed away, but I remained where I was, fascinated. She had already seen me do this, when I'd been on the beach; but it hadn't been ersatz sperm from a spray can that I'd rubbed between my labia and over my clitoris.

I licked my lips, remembering that during the passion of my arousal I'd also wiped semen over my mouth, then savoured its unique taste on my tongue.

'Hi,' Helen said, softly.

My gaze moved up from her foaming cunt to her eyes, and I saw that she was watching me. But her right hand continued moving, her fingers almost lost in the bubbles.

'I . . . ' I raised the comb, trying to explain what I was doing there.

98

'I got distracted,' Helen said, not caring that I was there.

I could still have turned and left, but I didn't. I wanted to watch.

Helen put down the spray can, picked up her glass of wine, which was again almost full. She took a long sip, then set the glass down. Meanwhile her fingers continued sliding up and down, in and out. Very reluctantly, she withdrew her right hand, and she wiped away the foam from her fingers by rubbing them across her breasts, smearing the bubbles over her nipples. She stood up, reached for the razor with her left hand, then leaned back against the basin.

'Here we go,' she said.

Her hand was absolutely steady. I was the one who was trembling as I watched her transfer the razor to her right hand. Slowly, she reached down to where her right leg met her crotch and carefully drew the blade across her pubis.

She left a diagonal track over an inch wide, like the path of a snowplough which had carved its way through a thick white drift. Then she ran her fingertips over the smooth flesh, and she smiled – and I remembered to breathe again. It was almost as if it had been happening to me: that she was a circus performer doing her act; that she was the knife-thrower and I was the girl with the blades flashing close by my naked flesh.

Rinsing the soap from the razor, Helen drew it across in the other direction, up from her right thigh, producing an X-shape across her pubic mound. A few more light strokes, first horizontal, then vertical – and her flesh was totally bare. She wiped her shaven skin with a towel, let the towel fall, and rubbed her fingers across her hairless pudenda.

'That feels nice,' she said, softly, 'really nice.'

Her eyes met mine, and for a moment I thought that she was going to invite me to feel her cunt. And

99

it seemed so natural, no different from examining any other part of her body, that I probably would have done. Then she frowned, and looked down.

My eyes followed the direction of her gaze, and I saw that her fingers were probing between her parted legs. I thought that she was going to start fingering herself again, but from her expression I soon knew that was not her intention.

'A girl's work is never done,' she sighed. 'Look.'

I looked, and my heart missed a beat as I gazed at Helen's twat. I could see her clitoris protruding from between her labia. My hand automatically went over my crotch, in case my own clit was in view – although I knew I was not yet excited enough for it to have become sufficiently erect, and even so it would have been masked by my blonde curls.

Helen was tugging at the hairs which grew upon her outer labia, and in doing so she had pulled back her cunt lips and thus revealed her clit. It was those hairs I was meant to be looking at.

'No one can see those,' I managed to say.

'You can see them,' Helen replied. 'If a job's worth doing . . . ' She reached for the aerosol can, aimed it upwards and sprayed another jet of foam between her thighs. 'Wow!' She offered me the can. 'Even if you won't shave, give yourself a spray. It's worth it.'

My heart was beating very fast, my nipples were fully dilated, the areolae very pink and standing out above my pale flesh. I could sense the moistness between my thighs, and I knew it wouldn't be too long before my inner labia began to swell and my clitoris to grow. I didn't need any more stimulation, and I shook my head.

All this time, I kept thinking: I shouldn't have been there; I shouldn't have been watching; I shouldn't have stayed. But I did.

I was mesmerized by what Helen was doing, and I watched as she picked up the razor once more, opened her thighs even wider, spread her twat flesh with her left hand, and prepared to glide the blade across her labia.

While I studied her foam-covered cunt, I realized that Helen was gazing at me.

'This is going to be difficult,' she said. 'I can't really see. Will you do it for me?'

She held out the razor towards me, and I found myself taking it, then going down on my knees in front of her bubbling crotch.

'No!' I said, as I managed to break the hypnotic spell. 'I can't!'

'You've cut my hair before,' said Helen. 'This is no different.'

The first part of what she said was true, and I tried to work out the flaw in her logic. Trimming an inch or two from her thick black mane, I reasoned, couldn't be compared with gliding a razor over her *labia majora*.

'This *is* different.' I gave her back the razor. 'Very different. I've never used a razor before. Would you trust me?' I nodded towards her vagina. 'There?' I looked up.

Helen met my gaze, studied the razor, reached for her wine and took a gulp, then said: 'No.'

She raised her left leg, resting it on the side of the bath, and I glimpsed a line of pink between the white foam. It was the cleft of her inner labia, eighteen inches from my eyes. I tried to get up, but my limbs refused to obey. All I could do was watch as Helen continued shaving her cunt. She did it very carefully, very slowly, until not a wisp of hair remained. To make sure there was nothing left, she ran her fingers over her labial folds, and I saw her fingertips lightly caress her clitoris.

For a moment I thought she was about to continue masturbating, to slide her fingers deep inside – and I didn't know whether I wanted her to or not. I felt both embarrassed by the idea, yet simultaneously very aroused. It was too late by now to leave the room, but it wasn't too late to start finger-fucking myself.

Suddenly I felt something cold against my right breast, and I leaned back. My attention had been so trapped by what Helen was doing to her twat that I hadn't noticed her reach for the shaving cream – which she had sprayed across my right boob. I'd pulled away instinctively, and now I lost my balance, slipped and fell onto my back on the bathroom floor.

Then Helen was across me, laughing as she pinned me down, and another streamer of foam spurted towards my chest. This time she encircled my left tit with a ring of thick bubbles. She aimed the aerosol at my nipple to complete her design, and I gasped with delight as the cold spray splattered across my sensitive skin.

I lay back, also laughing, as Helen constructed a pinnacle of foam, using my nipple as its foundation. It kept spiralling higher and higher above my breasts, until the aerosol was empty. Then Helen stopped giggling. I looked up at her, and she looked down at me.

She was perched above me, her outspread thighs above my hips – and her hairless cunt was directly above my hairy twat. She slowly lowered herself, until her smooth flesh was touching my pubic hairs. I lay absolutely still, making no response. She rocked her hips to and fro slightly, rubbing my hairs across her shaven skin. Then she lowered herself a little more, until her pubic mound was pressed against mine.

'What do you want to do?' Helen asked.

As she gazed down at me, I saw that her eyes were not properly focused. She was even more inebriated than I was, I realized.

I reached towards the foam which was piled upon my left boob, and I flicked some of it at her. The drops speckled her neck and breasts, and again I was reminded of a streak of semen. But Helen didn't move. Even when I scooped up a handful of thick white bubbles, she simply watched. Then I wiped them all over her face. She closed her eyes as I did so.

'I could do with a shower,' I said, and I smeared the rest of the foam across my ribs. 'A cold shower.'

Helen opened her eyes, and she yawned – and three holes appeared in the foam across her face. She reached for her glass of wine, draining it all in a single gulp.

'I think you're right,' she said, and she climbed off me.

I continued to lie on the ground, because that was a lot easier than getting up, and I watched as Helen stepped into the shower. I was very tempted to join her, but I thought it was safer to remain where I was. We'd gone much further than I'd wanted, but we had managed to retreat. This wasn't some fantasy from an erotic magazine, this was real life. We were still friends, no more than friends, and that was how I wanted it to be.

The next thing I knew, a spray of cold water hit me. 'Hey!'

'Wake up!' shouted Helen, as she turned off the shower spray. 'Your turn.'

I must have fallen asleep on the floor, and I got to my feet, water and shaving foam dripping down my body. Helen began to dry herself, and I took her place in the shower.

'Drying my hair always took the longest,' she said. 'But now I'll be dry in half the time!' She grinned as she patted her bare pubis.

I switched on the shower. At first the cold water was a shock, but after a few seconds I could feel the needle-sharp jets begin to invigorate me. It was almost as good as a swim. I could have slept no more than a minute or two, but that had been sufficient time for my ardour to diminish. Now my nipples grew hard again, but only from the cold spray which rinsed the foam from my torso. I turned my face up to the welcome water, allowing the icy drops to revive my body, to cool the last of my passion and dissolve the alcoholic haze which had dulled my senses.

'Shall I make some coffee?' asked Helen.

I spat out a stream of water. 'Yes.'

At last, reluctantly, I switched off the water and climbed from the shower. I didn't bother drying myself, because the sun would soon achieve that. Down in the kitchen, the coffee was bubbling away in the percolator. I went outside, expecting to find Helen. She wasn't there; she must have gone up to her room for something.

I lay back in my chair, luxuriating in the bright sunshine, watching as the drops of water evaporated from my flesh. I ran my hands through my hair, pushing it back behind my ears. Glancing towards the kitchen door, I fingered my damp pubic hairs. I liked them, I realized. I would no more cut them off than I would have shaved my head. Perhaps if they were another colour, I might have thought otherwise. I yawned and looked towards the kitchen, wondering why Helen hadn't come down again. The coffee must have been ready by now, and so I went inside, poured it into two mugs, then carried them upstairs and into Helen's room.

She was lying on the bed, naked, supine, asleep. She looked very young and innocent, although in the latter case appearances were deceptive.

I also felt like taking a nap, but I didn't want to lie down outside. I always had to be careful with my skin, and the suntan cream had been washed away by the shower. Never having been exposed to ultraviolet rays before, my boobs would soon become burned; and I could imagine what the sun would do to my nipples.

'Helen,' I said, quietly. 'Coffee.'

If she was deeply asleep, I didn't want to wake her. There was no response. I yawned again, putting the two coffees down on the cabinet by the bed as I wondered what to do. Then I climbed on to the bed and sat by her side. Many was the time we had been on this bed together, talking and talking – but we'd always had our clothes on.

'Helen,' I repeated. 'Coffee.'

I reached for my own drink, but it was too hot, and I put it back. I slid further down the bed, stretching out, and my hip came into contact with Helen's. Her skin was very warm. I became still immediately, but she didn't respond, and I lay down by her side. We were almost touching, my body a fraction of an inch from hers.

I gazed at her nude figure, able to study her for as long as I wanted. All I did was look, gazing at her breasts and her shaven pubis, but my nipples started to grow hard again as I studied her naked body.

As I examined her breasts, I remembered how she had licked at one of her own tits, sucking the nipple into her mouth. I touched both of my breasts, gently squeezing the hardness of my nipples between my fingers.

'Helen,' I whispered, and again there was no reaction.

I turned and leaned over her, my head descending towards her nearest breast. I kept my eyes upon her face, expecting that any moment she would open her eyes and start laughing.

But she remained almost totally still, only her chest rising and falling as she breathed in and out. I lowered my head to her bare boob, my tongue flicking out to caress the nipple, stroking lightly across the surface, then encircling the areola, before gently sucking the dimpled flesh into my mouth.

Helen had not responded, but her nipple did. I felt it begin to grow between my lips, starting to swell as I worshipped it with my mouth. I drew the nipple into my mouth, and it became even firmer against my probing tongue.

Then I drew back, gazing down upon what I had created. Helen's flesh was wet with my saliva, and my cunt was wet with my own juices. There was a slight smile on Helen's face, although I knew she was fast asleep. I wondered what she was dreaming.

I also smiled, and I fantasized about what I could do with Helen now that she lay nude in bed with me.

Instead, I rolled over and lay on my back, my side pressed up against hers. We were touching from ankle to thigh, from hip to shoulder. One of my hands rested lightly upon my cunt. That was all I wanted. I had no need of more intimate contact with myself, because I felt totally relaxed and content.

My other hand lay upon Helen's shaven twat, the middle finger over her cleft. Again, I required no more than that.

And so the first time I ever slept with someone else, that someone else was another girl.

Chapter Eight

Time went by: the hours and the days, the weeks and the months.

School started again, but Simon and Danny had left and were now working. I never saw Simon again, except as a passer-by, and Helen and Danny also soon parted. Neither did I ever see as much of Helen as I had on the day that she shaved off her pubic hairs, and nor did she ever see all of me again – at least not in the flesh. But I was so pleased when my first nude photographs were published that I gave her a copy of the magazine; she even asked me to autograph every page.

We were still friends and still went out together, although not so much as we used to; but neither of us ever referred to that summer day in her house. I didn't know if Helen kept her cunt smooth and hairless, or whether she'd allowed her pubes to grow back. But my own hair grew longer – the hair on my head.

Although Helen and I never spoke about what had happened, not that much *did* happen, I certainly thought about it – and what *might* have happened . . .

While we'd lain together during our wine-induced stupor, I'd dreamed that I was kissing a man with a beard. But I suspected that really the dream had been about kissing something else, that my mind had been conjuring up lesbian fantasies. The dream couldn't have been about Helen, I initially thought, because her cunt had been shaven. But dreams never make sense, and so Helen could well have been the subject of my dream. There wasn't any other girl I would have dreamed of; but at least I never dreamed of her again.

Then came the end of term and the Christmas

vacation. Once again, I worked at the same hotel for most of the holiday. Over the short Christmas season, the place was even busier than during the summer. It was almost as if the same number of people had to be catered for in a shorter space of time; that because there wasn't as much daylight during the winter, everything had to be condensed into fewer hours.

I didn't mind working during the winter, because I felt that I wasn't missing anything. I couldn't have been on the beach because it was too cold, and for the same reason I couldn't have gone swimming. During the grey months of winter, I only ever felt half-alive. Why hadn't I been born where it was hot all year? If I could have hibernated during winter, I would have done. Instead, I had to wrap up in thick, warm clothes and wait until the sun came out again.

Having been inside for so long, I felt as though I'd completely missed the summer. Whatever happened, I wasn't going to lose the next one. I was determined to find a job where I could work outside.

The hours at the hotel were longer during the winter, the work seemed harder, but the pay was as bad as it had been several months earlier. And then, as always happens, six days after Christmas Day it was New Year's Eve. I had expected to keep working until long gone midnight, but suddenly I realized that everything I needed to do had been done. There was no point in hanging around longer than necessary, and I wasn't paid by the hour, so I changed out of my work clothes and left.

It was 11.15 as I walked out of the back door; three-quarters of an hour until the new year. I'd been invited to a couple of parties but said that I couldn't make them because I had to work. There was still time to go to one of them, but I decided not to. Probably everyone else would have been out drinking and having fun before the party. I was totally sober, not really in the mood for celebrating.

I crossed the road from the hotel and stood by the rail on the promenade, looking down at the dark beach and the even darker ocean. It was hard to believe that I'd been swimming in there only a few months ago; it looked so cold and uninviting.

Tomorrow morning, there would be the annual New Year's Day swim, when a few of the local crazies went charging into the icy waters – and soon came rushing out again. The earliest I'd ever been in the sea had been on April the first. That had been two years ago, when Helen and I had tried to prove we were both April fools. The water had been cold enough then, so it must have been freezing now.

Helen would be at one of tonight's parties, with whoever it was she was fucking that week. I'd been out with a few other boys, but never had much enthusiasm for them. My sexual career had progressed no further. If anything, it had regressed. I'd had tongues down my throat, hands around my tits, but I hadn't let any of them get their fingers inside my panties. Neither had I jerked off any of my new companions.

I had, however, continued to explore the potential of my own cunt. Not a night went by without my fingers rocking me to sleep. Whenever I was naked, if I took a shower or a bath, I couldn't resist touching myself up. I would resist as long as possible, trying to build up the excitement so that its final release would be even more pleasurable.

After trying Helen's suntan cream, I experimented with several other creams and oils, first rubbing them over my nipples and breasts, only slowly sliding my fingers down towards my vulva. Sometimes I would let drops of body lotion fall onto my pubis, which would then drip down between my labia. Other times I would rub my fingertips over my outer lips, feeling them part at my touch. Then my fingers would glide within, across the inner labia, before finally homing in upon the most sensitive flesh of my whole being. By that stage, my clitoris would be craving my caress, and I would bestow all the intimate affection which it deserved. In return, it would share its splendid orgasm with the rest of my body.

But I didn't always need to touch my cunt to achieve a climax. Occasionally, I would comb out my pubic hairs as a prelude to masturbation, and on one memorable occasion the sensation was so exquisite that it was sufficient to give me a wonderful orgasm. Or by slowly stroking the rest of my body, developing an increasing awareness of every sensitive zone, by fondling my breasts and stroking my nipples, I could sometimes succeed in bringing myself off without my fingertips ever touching my clit.

And sometimes I couldn't – or wouldn't – wait. Without any mental anticipation, without any physical preliminary, my fingers would invade my twat, and on such occasions it was as if I were in a race, that I had to bring myself off as quickly as possible.

Different methods seemed appropriate at different times, and none could be described as better than the other – because they were all great!

I only ever used my fingers to stimulate myself, because there seemed an endless sequence of variations by which I could achieve my sexual peak. I could slip my hand between my legs, my palm pressing down on my pelvic bone, my index and third finger sliding over my outer labia, while the middle finger slipped deep within; or I could lick my index finger, then lightly glide it across the tip of my clitoris; or I could circle the knuckle of my thumb around my clit; or I could gently roll my swollen clit between my thumb and forefinger; or for variation I could use the fingers of my left hand to treat my twat; or else I could give myself the full treatment, using all eight fingers and both thumbs, each of them sliding over and rubbing against my hypersensitive cunt flesh.

When she was alone, with no cock to comfort her, I knew that Helen did not restrict herself to just her fingers. I had often heard her refer to her 'favourite' hairbrush, although I never saw her brushing her hair with it. I only knew what she meant the day that I saw her turn it upside down and kiss the handle; and in case she had not been sufficiently explicit, she then ran her tongue up and down its phallic shape.

Even after discovering this, I was not tempted to experiment. At that time, I believed there was only one thing I couldn't provide which should go into my cunt.

And that was probably next on my sexual agenda. The big one: losing my virginity.

As I gazed at the ocean, I thought that maybe that should be my new year resolution: at some time during the next twelve months I would fuck for the first time.

I smiled at the idea. My first fuck was something which would happen sooner or later, whenever the time was right, but I wondered about the kind of things which I couldn't predict. What would happen over the next year? Where would I be in exactly twelve months from now?

'Probably,' I said aloud, 'right here.'

It was a depressing thought. The summers had always been enjoyable, because of the sea and the beach. If all my future summers were like the last one, however, there would be very little time for lazing on the beach or swimming. And that was what seemed likely, because eventually I was going to have to work full-time. It was all a part of growing up, and I wasn't looking forward to it.

Perhaps that was why I was in no hurry to fuck. Maybe I considered that I could postpone growing up by remaining a virgin. I wanted to stay young, to be able to do crazy things like go for nude midnight

111

swims – because that wasn't the sort of thing which responsible adults ever did.

Without any conscious decision, I found myself heading down the flight of steps that led to the beach. I was used to walking over the pebbles and sand in the darkness, but I wasn't used to the cold. It wasn't cold enough yet for my breath to condense. The temperature would drop much more over the next couple of months, during January and February. That never made any sense to me, why it was always colder after mid-winter's day than before.

It was almost low tide, and I made my way slowly towards the edge of the ocean, then halted a few feet away from where the receding waves washed over the sands. The sea was relatively calm for the time of year, and the only sound was of the waves lapping around the girders of the pier fifty yards away. Had this been summer, the ocean would have been so inviting. I was curious about how cold it really was, but I didn't want to go any closer because my suede boots weren't made for beachcombing. So I unzipped them, removed my socks, rolled up the legs of my jeans, and walked towards the edge of the water.

'Not going swimming, are you?' said a voice behind me.

I spun around quickly, seeing the dark outline of a figure a dozen feet away. It was a man, I knew that from the voice; but he was silhouetted against the lights of the promenade, his face in shadow.

I didn't feel scared, only very surprised. If the man had meant me any harm, he wouldn't have announced his presence by speaking.

'What's it got to do with you?' I said.

'Everything,' he replied. 'I'm the lifeguard.'

'Lifeguard! In the middle of winter? In the middle of the night?'

'But what night is it?' he asked.

'New Year's Eve.'

'Exactly. And people do stupid things on New Year's Eve. They go to clubs, they go to parties, and they decide to see in the new year by going for a swim. Most of the people who drown late at night have been drinking. They go swimming because they've been drinking, and because they've been drinking they drown.'

By now my eyes had adjusted to the light, and I could see that the man was dressed completely in black – he was wearing a wetsuit. He was covered from head to toe, with only his hands and face visible. A pair of binoculars hung around his neck.

'So you're here to make sure no one drowns?' I said.

'That's the idea. And the best way to make sure no one drowns is to make sure no one goes in the water.'

'Even the sober ones?'

'It's not my job to stop them. If they're mad enough, they can go in.'

'I'm sober,' I said. 'I haven't been drinking.'

'I know, I can tell. But would you like a drink?'

'What? You're inviting me for a drink?'

'Almost.' He reached down to his side and pulled something from his belt. The moonlight reflected off its polished surface as he stepped closer. It was a hip-flask, and he offered it to me.

'Thanks,' I said, automatically accepting it, even though I wasn't sure I wanted a drink. 'What is it?'

'Taste it.'

I unscrewed the cap and sniffed at the contents.

'Don't be so suspicious,' said the lifeguard. 'You think it's drugged, that I'm going to abduct you and swim back to my submarine?'

'If I thought that, I'd drink it!' I laughed. Then I put the flask to my lips, tilted it back and swallowed a mouthful. The liquid burned its way down my throat, warming me immediately. I coughed, then handed it back. 'Thanks. What was it?'

113

'Rum,' he replied. 'Cheers. Happy New Year.' He took a long swig from the flask.

'Do you usually drink on duty?'

'Only for medicinal purposes.' He screwed back the cap and tucked the flask into his belt.

He was about six feet tall, with the long limbs and broad shoulders of a natural swimmer; and he must have been at least twice my age, perhaps even more.

I glanced around. 'Not many people here tonight,' I remarked.

'I hope it stays like that.' He reached for his binoculars and surveyed the beach in both directions.

'You can't see anything with those, can you?'

'Try them.' He took the binoculars from his neck and passed them to me.

They were very heavy, with wide lenses. I raised them to my eyes, focused on the pier – and it was almost as if the night had been banished. Everything was far lighter, and I could see much further. Details that would only have been visible during the day, which should have been hidden in the darkness, were suddenly visible. There was no real colour – it was almost like watching a black and white movie – but I was amazed by how well I could see.

'That's fantastic,' I said.

'Night glasses,' he explained.

'I bet you've seen all sorts of things with these.' I remembered what I'd got up to on the beach that summer, when I thought the darkness was hiding me – and I now wondered if anyone had been watching.

'All sorts of things,' the lifeguard agreed, as I handed the binoculars back to him. 'Anyway, what are you doing down here?'

'Just walking.' I looked down at my bare feet. 'I thought I'd see how cold the sea was.'

'Because you might go for a swim?'

I shook my head.

'I thought not.'

114

'What do you mean?' I asked.

'You don't look the type.'

'What type am I? The female type?'

He looked me up and down. 'Definitely – but not the type to go swimming at night.'

'Ha! I often go swimming at night.'

'Really? When did you last go in?'

'Er . . . three months ago.'

'Anyone can go swimming when it's warm.'

'And any drunk can go swimming when it's cold.'

He smiled. 'When I was a kid, I used to go swimming every day of the year.'

'Oh yeah? Where did you live? Hawaii?'

'Along the coast, ten miles away.'

'And you went swimming every day?'

He nodded. 'But kids these days, you just aren't tough enough.'

I liked the way he appeared to think I was a 'kid'; but I didn't like the way he appeared to think I wasn't tough enough. I turned and slowly walked into the sea. The water immediately froze my feet, and I clenched my teeth so as not to gasp at the shock. I kept going, taking several more steps until the water was almost level with my rolled-up jeans. As soon as I was used to the temperature, it didn't seem too bad. Perhaps, I reasoned, that was because my legs had grown numb.

'Come on in,' I said, looking around, 'the water's lovely.'

He laughed. 'Are you going for a swim?'

'I haven't got a towel,' I said, as I returned to the beach.

'I can lend you one.'

'Give me another drink, and I'll think about it.'

I thought that he would refuse, but he smiled and passed me his hip-flask. He had a nice smile, and I studied him as I took another gulp of rum. From what little I could see of him, he wasn't bad looking for such an old guy. I held the rum in my mouth for a few seconds, before allowing its fiery warmth to trickle slowly down my throat. He also took another swig when I handed the flask back.

'But I can't lend you a swimsuit,' he said.

'I don't usually bother with one. Not at night.'

'Yeah,' he said, making it obvious that he didn't believe me.

There was a very simple way of proving I was telling the truth, but I turned away from him and gazed out across the sea.

'Yeah,' I said. 'But don't let me keep you from your work. Thanks for the drink.'

'Happy New Year.'

'Happy New Year.'

I looked over my shoulder, watching as the lifeguard walked back down the beach, heading towards the pier. He was soon out of sight, lost in the darkness. I wondered what to do. I could simply put my boots back on and go home . . . or I could strip off and go for a swim. The lifeguard didn't believe that I would, or that I'd go in the water naked.

And so I started to undress.

I wouldn't have done so while he was near enough to see me, but now that he was gone I could pretend that I was alone. I knew he could see me through his night glasses, however – and he knew that I knew he could see me . . .

Taking off my jacket, I spread it out on the sand and began piling the rest of my clothes onto the lining. First my thick sweater, my blouse, and then my jeans, until all I wore were my briefs and short-sleeved T-shirt. There was a light breeze which had already produced goose-pimples all over my bare skin. My nipples were hard, pressing through the fabric of my T-shirt. I started to realize that this wasn't such a good idea; but having gone so far, I felt that I couldn't stop now.

116

My briefs would have been dragged off by the waves, but I considered keeping on my T-shirt, although not for reasons of modesty – I already knew I was doing this so that the lifeguard could see me in the nude, and perhaps to prove I wasn't as much of a 'kid' as I appeared. But I thought that the shirt might insulate me from some of the cold. Then I realized the sea was so icy that it would hardly make any difference. In any case, this wasn't a time for thought. I was wasting too much time, getting cold simply standing doing nothing. I had to act now, or else I never would.

So I quickly shed my shirt, peeled off my panties, and I ran into the water. It felt even colder than it had been a few minutes earlier, but I kept going, plunging through the sea until I was deep enough to dive head-long into the black waves. When I'd first tried the temperature, the coldness had numbed my feet. This time it again seemed as if all my nerve-endings had been anaesthetized. But as I began to swim, to use every muscle in my body, I became aware that the opposite was true – that my senses had been height-ened by the shock of the cold water. I felt absolutely alert, that my mind and body were as one, my physical peak perfectly complementing my total awareness.

This was no ordeal. It was great, I was really enjoy-ing myself, and I now felt warmer in the water than I had done naked on the beach. Why had I never swum in winter before? There was no reason why I couldn't do this every day of the year.

Swimming did seem a little harder than usual, but that could have been because I hadn't done it for three months. My limbs seemed to respond more slowly, and it was a greater effort to propel myself through the water, almost as if my body were growing heavier. I was slowly weakening, I realized. The icy ocean was draining all my strength. I'd been in the sea long enough, and so I turned and kicked my way towards the shore. When I reached the shallows, I got to my hands and knees. My whole body was shivering, my teeth were chattering.

'Another half a minute,' said the lifeguard, as he hauled me to my feet, 'and I'd have come and got you.'

'I was all right,' I insisted, pushing him away. 'I am all right.' I made my way onto the beach, hugging myself for warmth, and glanced around. 'Where are my clothes?'

'You should get dried first,' he told me.

My arms were folded under my breasts, but the lifeguard was looking at my face, not my bare boobs or the rest of my naked body.

'Where's the towel you promised me?'

'The pier,' he pointed. 'I'll get your clothes.' He started to walk away.

'Give me a drink first,' I said, and I hopped from foot to foot in the hope of warming myself up.

He turned, and now his eyes did focus on my naked boobs as they bounced up and down. He stepped towards me, reaching for the flask at his hip.

'Cold, are you?' He smiled and held out his other arm, curling it towards me.

I accepted the invitation, moving closer. His arm came down around my shoulder, cradling me, and his hand felt hot upon my freezing shoulders. I huddled up to his side, and even his wetsuit seemed warm against my bare flesh. I held out my hand for the rum, but instead he lifted the flask to his own lips and drank.

Then he lowered his head towards me, turning my body towards him, and instinctively I tilted my face up to meet his. We kissed. His lips were burning hot, mine were icy cold. His tongue probed between my teeth, my lips parted – and my mouth was instantly flooded by the rum which the lifeguard had been holding between his lips. His tongue stirred the liquid in my mouth, and I swallowed. The rum burned its way

118

down my throat, warming me from within. But his kiss was warming me even more.

He pressed my naked body close to him, interlacing his fingers beneath my buttocks and raising me up until my face was on the same level as his. And still we kissed, while my tongue explored his mouth, searching for any last drops of rum.

'Is that the kiss of life?' I asked, once our lips had finally parted.

'Yes. It takes years of training.'

'I think I'd like to learn,' I said, truthfully. I'd never been kissed with such passion, and it had nothing to do with the rum. That was just a bonus.

He lowered me onto the sand, and I shivered.

'Want to go back to my place?' he asked.

'So you can warm me up?'

'I think you are warmed up,' he said, and he smiled as his tongue touched his upper lip, perhaps tasting the salt that had been on my mouth.

'Where is your place?'

'The pier. I'll get your clothes.'

I hugged myself again while I watched him run down the beach, almost vanishing in the darkness. My mind was in a turmoil as I wondered what I should do, whether I ought to just pull on my clothes and head for home, or whether I should go with the lifeguard. It was evident that he wanted to fuck me.

And I'd no idea what it was that I wanted.

'Come on,' he said, as he returned, my bundled-up clothes tucked under his arm. 'You'll get pneumonia if you just stand there.'

I wanted to ask: *What would I get if I go with you?* But I remained silent. I could have been totally wrong. Maybe he was only going to offer me a towel, a place inside where I could get dry. He was supposed to be patrolling the beach; he didn't have time to do anything else. In any case, to him I was just a kid.

That wasn't what his kiss had said, however. There

had been so much promise in that lingering embrace, a tantalizing taste of what else a man of such experience had to offer me.

There was only one way to find out.

'Okay,' I said.

Side by side, we quickly walked towards the pier. He made no effort to touch me again. We reached a set of rusty steps which spiralled up around one of the legs of the pier. There was a sign across the handrail: *Danger. Keep Away.* He jerked his thumb upwards.

'You first,' I said.

I didn't want him below me, gazing up at my bare behind.

He ducked beneath the warning sign and started to climb, and I followed. The steps were very corroded, speckled with limpets and draped with seaweed. Instead of leading all the way up to the decking of the pier, the steps only went as far as a small platform several yards below.

'My office,' said the lifeguard, as he took my arm and helped me up the last few steps.

He gestured at the bare planks. Except for a large wooden box, there was nothing else, not even a raised lip of wood to form a token barrier around the edges. It was the ideal vantage point for him to survey the beach either side of the pier. He put my clothes into the box, followed by his night glasses.

'Where's this towel?' I asked, cupping my hands and blowing onto them.

'Here,' he said, as he pulled a huge towel from the box – and unzipped the front of his wetsuit.

He pushed back the hood of his suit and slid his arms free, and his body was still almost as dark. His arms and torso were matted with thick black hairs; the hair on his head was jet black, cropped short. He stepped towards me, one end of the towel held in each hand. Once he was near enough, he looped the towel over me and drew me closer.

Before we even touched, I could feel his warmth. My breasts pressed up against his torso, and his heat flowed into my body from his chest. He rubbed the towel up and down my back, my buttocks, the backs of my thighs and legs, and I held him close, my arms around his waist, the side of my face resting against his pectoral muscles.

I reached for the flask at his hip, unhooked it from his belt, unscrewed the cap, and took a drink. The rum coursed its way down my throat, reviving me, and I could feel my blood begin to flow faster through my veins. I took another mouthful, tilting back the flask until it was empty, and I raised my lips to his.

He unbuckled his belt, took the flask from my hand, threw them both behind him, and his mouth came down to meet mine. It was his turn to drink from my lips, and we kissed for a second time, our mouths pressed hard together, our tongues duelling, our teeth clashing.

My hands slipped down his back, inside the wetsuit, until I was holding his buttocks, feeling the heat radiate from his firm flesh into my hands and my arms, up through the rest of my body. Every moment I was becoming warmer, and no longer was I shivering, but the wetsuit prevented me from being in total physical contact with his lean body. My right hand moved around to the front, to start pushing down the suit from that side as well as the back. But I was unable to resist the temptation of the lifeguard's cock. I couldn't wait, and my hand slid down inside, searching for his hard male flesh.

And when my probing fingers discovered his knob, that was perhaps the biggest surprise of the night. The lifeguard didn't have an erection. His prick more than filled my hand, but it wasn't hard. As my hand encircled the hot male flesh, however, I could feel it begin to grow firmer.

All this time we were still kissing, and I was

breathing faster and faster. The flames of passion were beginning to engulf my body, while the temperature of my skin continued to rise and another part of my being was also starting to generate heat. I could feel desire beginning to burn deep within my cunt.

Letting go of his penis for a few seconds, I managed to push his wetsuit down over his hips. Now that it was free, the lifeguard's cock sprang up towards the vertical, and my right hand returned to its prize. It continued to grow, and my palm glided up and down, feeling the foreskin as it slid back over the smooth dome of the glans.

His kiss was delicious, but I longed for more. I wanted him to stroke my buttocks, to lick my nipples, to finger my twat. Instead, he did nothing except continue to rub my back with the towel – and continue to kiss me.

Then he even stopped the kissing, stopped the towelling. He glanced down at where I held his dick in my hand. My palm was gripping tightly, sliding up and down. I stopped and let go, because it wasn't the thing to do. He wasn't a boy, he didn't want to be wanked. He looked into my eyes, and I gazed up at him.

I licked my lips, then whispered: 'Yes.'

He stepped out of his wetsuit, then stretched the towel across the planks and ran his hand over it, smoothing out the creases. My heart thudding, my pulse racing, I lay down on the towel. I lay on my back, my arms by my sides, and I opened my legs and closed my eyes.

I felt both scared and excited. Although I was no longer shivering with cold, I could feel myself trembling with anticipation.

I was going to fuck.

I was going to be fucked.

And I didn't know what I should do, how I should respond. Would it hurt? His cock had seemed so huge, how could it possibly fit inside my cunt without causing pain? But I didn't care, all I wanted was to have him inside me.

A hundred random thoughts flickered across my mind, and then the lifeguard was by my side and every thought was banished. I gasped with delight as at last his tongue found my breasts. He licked my tits, sucking upon each nipple in turn, and I sighed with delight as his tender tongue worked its magic upon me. I still hadn't moved and I kept my eyes closed, enjoying the sensation, and the heat far within me became even more intense.

But all too soon his mouth retreated from my breasts. He must have been preparing to slide his shaft deep inside me, and my body became tense, waiting for him to mount me. Then I felt pressure upon my pubis, and I realized that he must have been using his hand. He parted my pubic hairs, and I widened my legs even further to welcome him – and I gasped at the touch of his fingertips upon my cunt.

His touch was so soft, seeming to caress every detail of the most sensitive part of my whole being, and I was no longer motionless. Almost against my will, my hips began to writhe with pleasure. I was no longer in control. The lifeguard was manipulating my whole body as surely and certainly as his expert fingers manipulated my clitoris.

The sensation was totally different from when I finger-fucked myself, and I wondered what technique he could be using. I reached down to touch his hand, so that I could follow his movements.

I'd been relying totally on my physical senses; that was all I needed. My mind had been switched off, or else I would have realized far sooner that he wasn't using his fingers . . .

My probing fingers didn't find a hand upon my twat – instead I found his face nuzzled between my thighs.

It wasn't his fingers which were stimulating me: it was his tongue!

He was licking my cunt.

I'd been spiralling towards orgasm, but the sudden realization of what was occuring brought me to an instant climax.

I cried out in absolute ecstasy as I came.

My whole body seemed to shake without control. My hands clutched the lifeguard's head, as if trying to push him even further and deeper into me.

I had gone from freezing to boiling within a matter of minutes, and every inch of my skin was damp with sweat.

When I finally became still, totally drained by the shattering orgasm which had overwhelmed me, I released his head. I could still feel his tongue lapping at my labia and circling my clitoris, as he supped at my love juices.

At last, he pulled away, moving on top of me, his legs between mine. I felt something else touch my cunt, and this time there could be no mistake: it was his cock which nuzzled against the wetness of my inner labia.

His face was above mine, and we gazed at each other. He smiled, so did I, and his lips came down to meet mine.

Several things happened almost simultaneously.

As we kissed, I noticed a strange flavour on his lips. I realized that it was the taste of my own twat. I sucked hungrily at his lips, savouring my own come.

His knob began to slide slowly into my vagina, and I thrust my hips upwards, pushing myself onto his shaft. Then it was in: we were as one.

And I came again, instantly.

My whole body was ablaze, caught up in an orgasmic inferno which consumed every atom of my being.

124

The lifeguard began to fuck me, his penis gliding out then in, out then in.

And the world lit up, the sky suddenly afire with all the colours of the rainbow.

As my hands clutched his back and my hips began to rise and fall to meet his thrusts, I gazed in disbelief at the pyrotechnics which had illuminated the heavens.

I'd read about such things as this in romantic novels, but I'd never believed they could be true. I still didn't.

Then in the distance I heard bells begin to ring, car horns to sound, ships' sirens to howl, people to cheer and shout.

'Happy New Year,' said the lifeguard.

Only then did I recognize what was going on all around me. The spectrum of exploding lights was the midnight firework display, and the reason for the cacophony of sounds was that the new year had begun.

'Happy New Year,' I replied, as we continued to fuck.

I closed my eyes once more, enjoying the sensation of his flesh upon mine, his knob sliding within me. He stroked my face with his fingertips, he licked my nipples, he kissed my neck, and he slowly transported me to another world, a land of absolute bliss.

I thought that it would not happen again, could not happen again, that it was impossible. But because he was so expert, because he seemed to fuck forever, fast then slow, hard then soft, for the third time I ascended towards paradise. The smouldering embers within my womb were rekindled by the sparks from his cock as it slid between my labia.

Then, after an eternity, he became totally still, his prick thrust as deep into me as possible, his whole body held as rigid as his manhood.

It was his turn to groan with ultimate triumph, and I felt the bursts of heat as his seed spurted into me, and yet again my core flared into incandescence, carrying me to the hedonistic heaven of my third orgasm.

This time the fireworks were within both of us, magnified and reflected from one to another, across body and spirit, illuminating both of us with the radiance we had created.

He sank down upon me, and we lay in each other's arms, our bodies still linked, both breathing heavily, our sweat intermingling, our heartbeats in perfect synchronization.

He kissed the tip of my nose. I tried to capture his lips with mine, but he shook his head, smiled and pulled away. He sat up, reached for his night glasses and studied the beach.

'I've got to go to work,' said the lifeguard.

He began to dress, and I watched as his cock vanished inside his wetsuit.

That was the last time I ever saw him. He never gave me his name – but he had given me so much more.

Chapter Nine

I went looking for him, of course.

After a night like that, there was no way that I was going to forget the lifeguard – but I never found him again. He must only have been there for that one night, in case his services were required to fish out any drunken revellers who decided to celebrate the new year by going for a swim.

I even sneaked away from work next morning to watch the local crazies go for their new year's swim, in case he had also been hired to keep an eye on them. But there was no sign of him.

In a way, I was glad that I never saw him again, that we'd had only that one perfect encounter. If we had met again, we would of course have fucked again, and it couldn't possibly have been as magnificent as the first time. Or at least that was what I told myself. I didn't want to consider the possibility that it could have been even *better*, and that I'd never have the opportunity to find out.

There was always the summer. I wondered if he might return to patrol the beaches later in the year.

By then, however, I didn't care. The lifeguard had been the ideal teacher. He had given me my first lesson in fucking, but his wasn't the only cock in the world. And now that I knew what my cunt was really for, there was no stopping me . . .

Helen and I still went out together at least once a week, usually to a nightclub. The recent pattern had been that we would go there together, she'd find someone that she fancied, leave with him, and I'd have to make my own way home. That was okay by me. We always had some fun and a few drinks, we'd dance and laugh – then Helen would discover some-one new to fuck her.

For me, that was always the end of the night. I'd say goodbye to whoever I'd danced with, whoever had bought me drinks, maybe do some kissing and groping, but then I'd head for home. It only took half an hour to walk back, and I'd always declined the various offers of lifts – partly because it would prob-ably have taken much longer getting home by car, and partly because I didn't want to become involved.

Perhaps the way I acted was a reaction against Helen's behaviour. With her, it was a new guy every time. I didn't want every man – I wanted one man. Or so I believed. I still had romantic illusions, believing that one day I would discover my ideal partner, the man I would be with for the rest of my life. We'd meet, fall in love, marry. He'd be the only one for me, the one to whom I surrendered my virginity. As soon as I saw him, I'd recognize him; I don't know how I'd know he was the one, but maybe bells would ring.

It was too late for all that now, I supposed. My virginity had gone – and bells *had* rung, although the two were entirely unconnected.

There was far more to life than stories of ideal romance. They were about as realistic as fantasy worlds where beautiful damsels were rescued from perilous fates by handsome knights. Such imaginary heroes were always great warriors, armed with power-ful swords which they wielded so expertly. And it was obvious what those swords really represented.

This was the real world. I didn't want symbolism. I wanted the real thing. I wanted a man, and I wanted what a man could give me: his cock.

I spent a long, lonely week, and all that kept me going through the cold January nights were my own fingers and the hot memories of the lifeguard and the wonderful world he had opened up to me: the true world which I had sublimated for too long. It was time

128

for living, not for reading. I had to discover everything for myself, not absorb formula imagery which was only a pale reflection of true experience. My intellect had to become secondary to the instincts of my body.

And so a week into the new year, Helen and I went out to a club together. The evening began as usual. I always arrived with the sole intention of enjoying myself for the few hours that we were there, but Helen was always looking beyond that: her true enjoyment would begin once she had left. She had begun to fulfil her inner desires earlier than I had, and for that I envied her.

I was determined to make up for lost time. Instead of looking out for a few guys who were good to dance with, or who would at least buy the drinks, I was instead searching for one particular partner: someone I wanted to fuck.

There was no hurry, I knew. I didn't have to screw the first one to offer me a drink. There would be plenty of choice. If I wished, I didn't have to screw any of them. This was my first night out after having been initiated as a woman. I kept telling myself that there was no rush. There would be plenty more nights, plenty more men, plenty more fucks.

Every man in the club had the necessary equipment, and there was no way of telling in advance how good they were with it. Neither did I have to decide, I realized. Once again, I was thinking too much – and that was the last thing which was required. All I had to do was take things as they happened, one step at a time.

It was a very strange evening. Perhaps there had been other nights when nobody approached me for a dance, or offered to buy me a drink. If so, I'd never noticed before. I'd always been happy to dance by myself, and if I wanted a drink then I could buy one. I had never previously gone to a club with the intention of meeting a man; and now that I had done, they all seemed to be avoiding me.

As usual, Helen had picked up a guy – who probably thought that he'd picked her up. They danced and laughed and drank and talked. Until that night, I'd never been so conscious of being alone in the middle of a crowd.

Tonight was supposed to be my choice: that if I wished, I would choose someone to fuck; that if I didn't, I wouldn't. But it seemed that the choice was being forced upon me. If there was no one available, that meant there was nobody to fuck. It wasn't right that I should be denied the opportunity to decide. So if no one found me, then I had to find them.

It wasn't as if every man in the place was already spoken for. There were plenty of guys on their own or with their male friends, but there were also plenty of girls who had not paired off. I wasn't the only one by myself, although I felt as though I was.

I made my way towards the spiral staircase which led up to the bar on the balcony. The bottom of the staircase was a favourite place for the guys to stand, so they could look up the girls' skirts – and all the girls knew this. There was another bar; they didn't have to climb the wrought iron steps. But the balcony was also a favourite location, for everyone, because you could look down on the rest of the club and see everyone else.

I'd stood at the lower end of the staircase, and how much leg and thigh would be revealed depended on how long your skirt was, how flared, and how careful you were at climbing the stairs. Going up the spiral steps was all part of the game, and I knew exactly how to proceed in order almost to show off my panties.

A free bottle of 'champagne' was on offer to any girl who climbed the stairs without wearing any undies. The idea, of course, was that they should reach the balcony having made it very evident that they were wearing absolutely nothing underneath. There were always guys below who were willing to act as judges. Their cheers, whistles and applause were verdict enough for the awarding of a bottle of sparkling wine.

I felt their eyes gazing up at me as I climbed towards the balcony, but there was to be no prize for me. Although I wore no bra, I'd never considered doing without my knickers in public. That came later . . .

When I reached the balcony, I gazed down onto the crowd below. I felt more eyes studying me, but when I glanced towards the bar there seemed to be no one who was staring at me. Turning around again, I took my mirror from my shoulder-bag and pretended to be checking my lipstick. I saw a man's reflection studying me. When I turned, he had already looked away. He was at the far corner of the bar, and I made my way in that direction.

He must have been a couple of inches shorter than me, perhaps a couple of years older. He was nothing special, but he was the only person who had paid me any attention all evening. I stood next to him, waiting to be served – and waiting for him to offer me a drink. I gave my order, and I noticed him watching me from the corner of his eye. He was nervous, I realized, too shy to speak up and offer to buy my drink. It seemed the first move would have to be mine.

I glanced around quickly, and he was unable to look away in time: his gaze met mine. 'Would you like a drink?' I asked.

'Er . . . me?'

'Yes,' I replied. 'You.'

'Er . . . a drink?'

'Yes.' I gestured to his half-empty beer glass. 'One of those things.'

'Er . . . '

I decided for him. 'And the same again for him,' I told the barman.

I took out my purse. He still didn't offer to pay, so I bought the drinks.

'Er . . . thanks.'

'Cheers,' I said.

'Er . . . cheers.'

I wondered if I was wasting my time as well as my money, but then he suddenly smiled. I've never been able to resist a nice smile. I gave him my name, and he told me he was called Bruce. It was the first time he didn't say 'er . . . '

We started talking. Or rather, I started talking, and gradually the monologue turned into a conversation. We talked about everything and nothing, then Bruce bought us both another drink, and we continued talking about nothing and everything. Then he bought more drinks and we went down to the dance floor. Bruce was probably the worst dancer I've ever seen. He had absolutely no idea of rhythm, and he danced exactly the same way no matter what the tempo of the music. If I'd had any less to drink, his lack of ability would probably have embarrassed me. But he was enjoying himself, and his enthusiasm was infectious.

What bothered me most was that if Bruce was so bad at dancing, what was he like at fucking? According to legend, the way a guy performed on the dance floor was in exact correlation to his sexual expertise. Was I to go from one extreme to the other? From the lifeguard to Bruce? Although I'd earlier decided that I didn't have to fuck if I didn't want to, I was now certain that I wanted to. My cunt craved a hard cock, and Bruce was my only option.

When it was time to leave, I found Helen and her new friend almost fucking in the doorway. Although she kept boasting about her sexual athleticism, we both knew that she wildly exaggerated her exploits. She would tell stories to shock and amuse me, but I was more easily amused than shocked. Then she would interrogate me, asking when I was going to get myself screwed, warning that I was in danger of becoming an old maid. I'd protest that I was a young maid.

But that was no longer the case. I hadn't told Helen about the lifeguard. Not yet. Perhaps I would reveal all in time, but for the moment the fact that I was no longer a virgin was my secret. Or so I thought. Could it be that somehow Helen knew? Did it show? Did I look different? That was impossible, I knew, but perhaps some indefinable difference could be detected.

Could people tell I was no longer a virgin? Did they know it was only a week since I'd first been fucked? Was it something which only other women were aware of, because they had been similarly initiated?

I waved to Helen as Bruce and I passed by, and behind her guy's back Helen raised her forearm in a phallic gesture. I wasn't sure whether she was referring to herself, that she was about to score again, or whether she was wishing me luck. Perhaps both.

Then Bruce offered me his hand. I took it, thinking he wanted to hold it, but instead he shook my hand.

'Thank you for a very nice evening,' he said.

He was saying good-night; but as far as I was concerned, the night hadn't yet begun. I kept hold of his hand, making sure that he didn't escape.

'Have you got a car?' I asked.

'Yes, but I think I've had too much to drink. I was going to leave it in the car-park.'

'Aren't you going to give me a lift home?'

'Shall I call a taxi for you?'

'No,' I said. 'I'd rather you gave me a ride.'

Bruce looked at me and blinked, wondering if I meant what he thought I meant.

'Have a good time,' said Helen.

We turned as she and her friend went past, heading towards his car. I wasn't sure whether they were trying to hold one another up, or get inside each other's clothing. Perhaps both.

I'd lost count of the times I'd been offered a lift home. I'd declined every such offer, even the genuine ones. The one time I would have accepted, it seemed I wasn't even being asked. But I was determined that Bruce wouldn't evade me. Like it or not, I was getting into his car.

I wrapped my arms around myself, hunched up my shoulders, and said: 'It's cold out here. Why don't we get into your car to keep warm?'

We walked to his car and got inside.

'Okay,' Bruce said. 'I'll take you home. Where do you live?'

'I'll give you directions.'

He started the engine, and I navigated.

'I didn't realize you lived out of town,' he said, ten minutes later, as we headed out along the coast road.

'I don't. But we might as well take the scenic route. You're not in any hurry, are you?'

'I suppose not,' he said, and I directed him off the main highway and along the cliff road.

'Turn here. Along to the end. And . . . stop.'

We had to stop, because we had reached the end of the car-park. A few yards further was the edge of the cliffs. Beyond that was nothing – except the ocean, two hundred feet straight down.

'What are we doing here?' asked Bruce.

'Admiring the view.'

'But it's dark. There's nothing to see.'

I turned to face him, wondering if I was going to have to make the first move again.

'What do you suggest we do?' I asked. 'You want to go back?'

He looked at me. He shook his head. He smiled. He leaned towards me.

We kissed, and he kissed very hard, his tongue thrusting, his lips pressed tight up against mine. One of his hands held the back of my head, in case I should try to escape. His other hand was working on the buttons of my coat. I could have helped, had it undone in a moment, but I decided that this should be his move.

Once he'd managed to unfasten the buttons, his hand found my left breast, enveloping it with his fingers, his palm rubbing against the nipple. Then he began to work on the buttons of my blouse. There were lots of buttons, and at the rate he operated it would take quite a while even to undo enough to slip his hand inside. While I was waiting, I unzipped his pants and pulled out his erect knob.

Bruce stopped kissing me, pulled away and stared down. My hand was encircling his cock, feeling it pulse with vitality. I rubbed my thumb over the glans and felt the foreskin retract even further as his prick became more swollen.

'Nice cock,' I said to him. And it was: long and thick and meaty.

'Er . . . ' It was his first 'er' in a long while.

He glanced around, staring out of the windows. The glass was already steaming up. There were no other cars nearby. If any arrived, we'd see the headlights.

'Relax,' I said.

I tightened my grip on his dick, and I slid my hand up and down slowly. Bruce smiled, and his smile turned into a grin. He thought I was going to jerk him off, but that wasn't my plan. I let go of his solid flesh, and I quickly undid all the buttons of my blouse, exposing my bare boobs. Bruce gazed at my breasts, and he licked his lips.

'Get your pants down,' I told him.

'What?'

'You heard.' I pushed my blouse and coat off my shoulders, and was naked to the waist.

He started to reach towards my tits, but I leaned back slightly, letting him know that he first had to do as I asked.

135

'Maybe it would be easier if we got into the back of the car,' I suggested.

There were two seats at the front, with the hand-brake in between, and the steering wheel didn't allow Bruce much room for manoeuvre. The car was no wider at the rear, but there was one continuous seat without any obstruction.

'What for?' he asked, although he started to wriggle out of his pants.

'So we can fuck, of course.'

He froze and stared at me. 'Fuck?'

'Yeah. It's when one of *those*' – I tapped the tip of his dick with my forefinger – 'goes into one of *these*.' I raised my hips, lifted my skirt, thumbed down my panties, patted my pubis.

Pushing my undies all the way down, I kicked off my shoes, then climbed over onto the back seat. All I had on was my skirt and thigh-length cotton stockings. I sprawled across the back seat and tugged my skirt up around my waist, then I raised my index finger and beckoned to Bruce.

He had only unfrozen enough to turn his head, and his eyes were focused on my blonde curls. It was cold on the back seat, although one particular point of me was growing warmer. But I needed Bruce and his penis to turn up my internal heating to the maximum.

'Come on,' I said.

He did. He clambered over the front seat, his pants around his knees, his cock looking even more tempting now that it was totally free.

I spread my legs and slid up against the side of the car. Bruce knelt in front of me, and his hands came down upon my bare breasts. He lowered his head, sucking at my left nipple, while his fingers massaged my right boob. As always, it felt great having my tits licked and stroked. Gradually, Bruce became more horizontal, until he was almost on top of me. That meant he had to remove one of his hands, leaning on the floor to support his weight. His other hand also moved away, sliding down my body until it brushed across my pubic hairs. Then his fingers continued their southerly quest, down towards my vulva. But I needed no stimulation. I was already wet and waiting, and I grabbed his prick, guiding him towards me.

'Oh,' said Bruce. 'Oh, oh, oh, oh . . . '

The end of his knob glided across my swollen clitoris and I sighed with pleasure, then directed it between my *labia minora*. I shuddered in anticipation as I let go of his cock. Bruce thrust forward – and his shaft was driven deep inside my trembling twat.

'Oh, oh, oh, oh . . . '

I rocked my hips slightly, enjoying his hard maleness within my female flesh.

'Oh, oh, *oh, oh* . . . '

Bruce still hadn't moved, I realized. He'd pushed his tool all the way into my cunt, and it still lay buried there.

'Fuck me,' I whispered. 'Fuck me!'

'*Oh, oh,* OH, OH, *OHHHHHHH!!!!!!*'

And that was when I realized that Bruce *had* fucked me. I felt his penis twitch as he spurted his seed deep inside me, but it wasn't enough to make me come.

I looked at him, he looked at me.

'Sorry,' he said, shrugging slightly. 'I'm not . . . er . . . not used to . . . er . . . this . . . er . . . girls like you.'

'Shut up and keep still,' I told him, grabbing him with both arms and hugging his body close to me.

While his tool was still inside me, before it became detumescent, he was still of use. I rocked my hips up and down in small fast movements, rubbing Bruce's cock against my clit, sliding my labia over his hot flesh. I began to absorb his heat, the fires within growing more and more fierce, until suddenly the flames erupted, and the blaze brought me to my climax.

I gasped with ultimate satisfaction, my arms

releasing Bruce. He pulled away, freeing his cock from the prison of my cunt – and I guessed that he had never been such a willing captive, never held in such delightful confinement.

'A girl like me?' I asked.

'Er . . . I've never done it before . . . er . . . like this . . . er . . . in a car.'

'With a girl like me?'

'There aren't any girls like you.'

He knew exactly what to say, and I laughed.

'How many times have you done it?' I asked.

'All together?'

'Yes.'

'Including this time?'

'Before this time.'

'Approximately . . . er . . . zero.'

I smiled. Bruce was a virgin. Or had been until a minute or two ago.

'So that was your first fuck?'

He nodded.

'That's okay. We've all got to start somewhere. You didn't do so bad for a beginner.'

'Really?'

'Really,' I said. 'With a girl like me, I'm surprised you didn't cream yourself ages ago . . . '

He also smiled, and I reached for his cock. It was still half-erect, wet with my come. At my touch, it began to stiffen again.

'Do you want seconds?' I asked, rhetorically.

And so we did it again, and this time I achieved orgasm before Bruce did. This was one of the advantages of fucking a young man, I later discovered. They might not possess much in the way of technique, but what they did have was fast powers of recovery. They could get it up again very quickly.

The lifeguard had given me my first lesson in the ancient art of fucking, and then it had been my turn to teach Bruce. But in reality, that was all part of my own education. I learned as much from Bruce as he learned from me. And I've never stopped learning; there's always something new to be discovered.

Bruce and I were to do a lot of learning together over the next few months. It wasn't that I went cock-crazy, because compared to many of the girls I knew my behaviour was very restrained. I was a one-man girl, and for a long while Bruce was the only man for me. I wanted to fuck, and all I needed was one guy, one prick. So far as I was concerned, it seemed the perfect arrangement. I didn't have to keep finding someone new each time, and Bruce appeared to be more than content with our relationship. We'd meet up, go out in his car, and then we'd screw each other until we were totally shagged out.

We were limited by the dimensions and facilities of what we called the 'fuckmobile', but this became more of a challenge than a restriction. We kept discovering new positions in which to carry out our sexual experiments, then finding variations on these. Front seats, back seat, we did just about everything and anything that two people could do to each other inside a car. Bruce would sit on the front passenger seat, and I would be across his lap, while his cock was in my cunt. Sometimes I would face him, sometimes we would both be facing forwards. Then we'd try out the back seat, sometimes with Bruce kneeling between my thighs. Other times I would be the one kneeling, and he'd slide his dick into my twat from the rear, his balls slapping against my flesh as he fucked me.

I had some great times in that car, great times and great climaxes. I never regretted any of what happened, although Bruce and I had nothing going for us except that we liked to screw each other. That was okay for a while, but it was no basis for a long-term relationship. We seldom went anywhere, we rarely did anything else, we hardly ever talked – all we did together was fuck.

'Why don't we do it outside?' I suggested.

The months had gone by, it was no longer so cold, and there was no reason why we should confine our fucking to the car. The vehicle was parked above the cliffs. We were both naked, and I was sitting on Bruce's lap. We were playing with each other's genitals, teasing one another.

I glanced out of the window. It was a cloudy night, but the moon was low on the horizon and could also be seen reflected in the sea.

'What for?' asked Bruce.

'For a change,' I said, and I opened the door, climbed off his lap and out of the car. I knelt down, feeling the ground. It didn't seem too cold or damp. 'I've never done it on the grass.'

'A girl like you?' said Bruce, as he reluctantly left the car. 'Never fucked on the grass?'

I laughed. 'Let's do it,' I said, and I lay down, spreading my legs. 'Now.'

'My cock is at your command,' said Bruce, and he joined me.

We joined each other. His prick slid into my cunt and our hips began to rock: together, our loins firmly glued; in opposition, so that his shaft almost escaped my tight twat. The friction we generated began to heat my very core, the fires radiating through my veins.

Then Bruce suddenly became still. I didn't understand why, because I knew that he hadn't climaxed.

'It's raining,' he complained.

I kept thrusting my hips up, sliding his rigid knob between my labia. Bruce resumed shafting me, faster and faster. He seemed to have lost all genuine enthusiasm, and instead was in a hurry to get it over with. He exploded within me, and his ejaculation sparked off my own detonation. I twisted and writhed as the rapture enveloped me, gasped and moaned as I was ecstatically elevated to the highest level of bliss.

'It's raining,' Bruce repeated, as he rapidly withdrew and retreated to the car.

'So?' I said, as the cold rain danced across my naked body. I opened my mouth, catching as many drops as I could, and I ran my hands across my body, stroking my breasts, imagining that the rain was sea-water and that I was on the beach.

'I hate the rain,' Bruce told me.

'It'll soon be summer,' I said.

'I hate the summer.'

'We can go to the beach.'

'I hate the beach.'

'We can go swimming.'

'I hate the sea.'

That was when I finally realized we had absolutely nothing in common, nothing except fucking. And after tonight, I knew, we wouldn't even have that.

I stretched out on the grass, my arms high above my head, my legs wide apart. The rain cascaded down onto my nude body, and I thought about the summer which was to come: the sun, the sea, the sand.

And the sex . . .

141

Chapter Ten

'How much you make is entirely up to you. The more you sell, the more you earn. In theory the more hours you put in, the more you'll earn. It doesn't always work like that, of course. If it's raining, you'll sell nothing. If it's a boiling hot day, you'll make a fortune. And there are of course other ways of boosting your earnings. If you give small measures, they go further and you make more. If your arithmetic isn't so good, and you don't give the right change, again you make more. But the great advantage is that there's no one looking over your shoulder, telling you to get back to work, so if you get bored you can lock up and go for a swim.'

It was my first day in my new job. School was over – forever. Depending on my exam results, I'd be going on to college or looking for permanent employment. The main attraction of the former was that it would take me out of town, although now that it was summer I was happy to stay there for a while. Until then, I needed a temporary job, and this year I'd found one where I could work outdoors.

I was selling ice creams. I had a three-wheeled bike with a huge chill cabinet mounted on the front, and my job was to cycle up and down the promenade in search of customers. Cold drinks, frozen ices, several varieties of ice cream, I sold them – or hoped that I would.

'I know how well you can do here. You have to watch out for the police, because technically you aren't supposed to cycle along the prom. Being a girl, you should be okay. Just stick out your tits and give them a smile.'

He looked at me, as if expecting me to practise. I sat still in the saddle, not smiling.

'You'll also sell more if you smile,' he said.

'And stick out my tits?' I asked, and I smiled at him.

His name was Nick, and he used to go to my school. He had been one of the sporting heroes, having captained the football team the year they won the cup. He had been two years ahead of me, and I remembered how all the girls fancied him. Lithe and athletic, curly hair almost as fair as my own, baby blue eyes, Nick was very good-looking – and he knew it. He also had brains enough to leave town, which he'd done by going away to college. He only returned for the summer.

'Yeah,' said Nick, and he smiled as he studied my boobs.

I was wearing a white T-shirt and red shorts; that was all. No bra, no knickers, no sandals. The only other thing I had was a money-pouch on a belt round my waist.

'If I can earn so much,' I asked, 'why aren't you on the bike?'

Nick was wearing even less than I was, only a pair of swimming trunks and his money-pouch. But he had to carry a huge tray, which hung from a strap around his neck. It was insulated, lidded, and loaded down with almost as many drinks and ice creams as I had on the tricycle.

'I've done that for years,' he replied. 'I must have cycled hundreds of miles up and down the prom. I was fed up, and it will make a change operating on the beach.'

I glanced up at the clear blue sky. It was ten o'clock in the morning and already warm.

'It's a great day,' I said.

'You mean: a great day for selling ice cream! Good luck. See you later.'

'See you.'

143

I studied his firm buttocks as he turned and walked down the steps towards the beach. I'd already noticed how well he filled the front of his swimsuit, which was obviously why he wore it. Naturally, I wondered how long it would be before I'd have the chance to examine the contents in more detail, because I'd recognized the predatory look in Nick's eyes while he had been telling me about the job. This didn't seem to be the kind of occupation in which we shouldn't mix business and pleasure. I already knew that we would fuck, that Nick's would become the third cock to enter my cunt and my life.

But I wasn't going to let him think that I was easy; I intended to take my time before letting him inside my shorts. By the end of the first week's work, however, I realized that Nick must also have been playing hard to get. I'd hardly ever seen him, except when we happened to be back at the kiosk at the same time, refilling our coolers with more supplies. This was the souvenir stall at the entrance to the pier, and we worked for the man who owned it. We bought our supplies from him, and the difference between what we paid him and what we took from the customers was our earnings. I also had to pay for hiring the tricycle, which could have been one reason why Nick preferred carrying the tray: it was cheaper.

Originally, I hadn't approved of Nick's advice on how to make more money. I wasn't going to cheat anyone by giving small measures, or rob anyone by giving the wrong change. But at the end of the first day, having sold hundreds of ice creams and drinks, I had earned exactly . . . nothing.

Somehow, I was the one who'd been cheated and robbed. I suspected that some of this was the fault of the man who had hired me, that he hadn't supplied me with as many cones and cans as he claimed. From then on, I checked each item and kept a proper count of everything.

I'd also been cheated by the customers. At the end of the first day there were all kinds of foreign coins in my pouch, which could only have come from the language students. Others had pretended not to understand our currency, deliberately giving me the wrong money. Or else a group of them would crowd around the trike, pointing at what they wanted, then changing their orders, sometimes even helping themselves.

From then on, I was always careful with the foreign students; and the next day I made up for what I had lost on the first. But they weren't the only ones who had given me trouble. Some of those on holiday had also paid for less than they bought, a few of them claiming I'd given the wrong change. I thought that I must have been mistaken, and I paid up; but they had been deliberately robbing me.

To make up for this, I recycled all the foreign coins I'd collected and also made a few 'mistakes' with the change. Halfway through the first week, I estimated that I was back to what I should have earned. I could have kept on operating like that, but I didn't really want to keep making extra money in such a fashion.

Instead, I came up with a more legitimate method to charge higher prices. I made up my own stickers to cover the real prices on the front of the trike. Before returning to the kiosk, I always peeled off the stickers. It wasn't that the 'boss' would have cared – but he would have started charging me more for my supplies, and probably for using the icemobile.

'What a great idea!' said Nick, when he saw my price stickers. 'I thought I knew it all. Why didn't I ever think of that?'

I was on the promenade a mile from the pier, and he had suddenly appeared next to me. He was still in his tight swimming trunks, his money-pouch slung across his hip, but there was no sign of his ice cream tray.

'Can I steal your idea?' he asked.

'Can I stop you?'

He grinned and shook his head. 'I was down on the beach when I saw you, and I wondered if you wanted to go for a boat trip.'

'Maybe,' I said.

'How long have you been working? Eight days without a break? Lock the trike. Take an hour or two off.'

'Where's this boat?'

'There.' He pointed down to the beach, to where a fibreglass dinghy was half out of the water. 'It belongs to a friend.'

'Where's he going?'

'He's going nowhere. I've borrowed the boat.'

'So where are you going?'

'What is this? We can go wherever you want. Along the coast. Out to sea. I don't mind. I don't care. I just thought I'd ask you, that's all. If you don't want to go' – he shrugged and started to turn away – 'forget it.'

'Could we go swimming?'

He turned again. 'Yeah.'

As a kid I used to love diving into the water from a boat, but it was a long time since I'd been out in one.

'Okay,' I said, and I climbed from the saddle and chained the trike to the promenade rail. I locked the cooler box. 'Let's go.'

'What about your swimsuit?'

'I'll just wear a smile,' I said.

Nick stared at me, obviously not knowing whether to believe me.

'Come on,' he said, and we headed down the steps to the beach and towards the boat.

I knew that Nick had been watching me. He must have been waiting until I rode by, so that he could ask me to join him for a boat trip. But he had also been watching me for longer than that, because he knew I had a swimsuit. I kept it, a towel and a few other

146

things in a plastic bag inside the cooler. I hadn't worked eight days without a break. At least once a day, I'd locked up the icemobile and gone swimming. Nick knew this, and now he'd made his first move.

I wasn't sure what my own move would be, whether I really planned to go swimming in the nude. If I did, that would be an obvious invitation to fuck – although it was probably Nick's intention that he should shaft me out in the boat. I tried not to think ahead; I'd take things as they happened.

My usual routine was to lock my money-pouch inside the cooler box, and to hang the keys around my neck while I was swimming. As we walked across the sand, I realized that I was still wearing the belt, and I dropped the keys into the pouch.

When we reached the boat, I saw that Bruce's ice tray was on board, under the seat at the stern. It wasn't the kind of thing he could lock and chain to a railing. We pushed the dinghy into the sea. Nick held the craft steady while I climbed on board, and he followed. He used a paddle for the first fifty yards, until we were away from the swimmers, then he tilted the prop shaft of the outboard into the ocean, yanked on the cord and the engine roared into life. I went and sat on the seat in the bow, trailing my fingers in the water as we headed out to sea.

I pretended that I was on an ocean cruiser, embarking on a voyage around the world. All I could see ahead of me was the sea – and it stretched on for hundreds of miles, thousands of miles. Almost every land, every exotic country I had ever heard of could be reached by sea. Growing up on the coast, it was as if every other continent was so much nearer. To reach them, all you had to do was step into a boat and keep on going.

And I wished that I could keep on going, could continue sailing away, on and on until we made landfall upon some distant tropical beach.

All too soon, Nick switched off the outboard. The bow wave disappeared and the prow of the dinghy settled down, no longer riding across the waves. The craft began drifting, carried by the tide instead of by its own forward momentum.

I heard a splash, and I glanced quickly around. Nick had dropped the anchor. I looked beyond him, surprised at how far from the coast we appeared to be. We were less than two miles out, but the land seemed so insignificant, low and distant on the horizon.

I gazed up into the clear sky. Far above, there was a line of white, the contrail from a jet plane. I wondered what its destination could be. It would take weeks to sail to another continent; an aircraft could fly thousands of miles in a few brief hours.

'Like to be up there?' asked Nick. It was the first time either of us had spoken since we had left the shore.

'I don't know,' I said, and I didn't. 'I've never been in an airplane.'

'It's the best way to fly.'

I said nothing, watching as the vapour trail faded from the sky.

'Have you heard of the mile-high club?' asked Nick. 'It's made up of people who have fucked in airplanes.'

'So?'

'Want to join the mile-out club?'

I glanced down at the wooden decking of the boat. It was covered with mud and sand, the bilges awash with sea-water.

'This is your idea of seduction, is it?' I asked. 'All you do is say the word, and you expect me to lie down there and let you fuck me?'

Nick shrugged. 'Well, if you put it like that . . . yes.' He grinned at me.

'Thanks for the offer. It's hard to resist – but you aren't.'

148

He shook his head slightly, as if he couldn't believe what he'd heard.

'What happens to me now?' I asked. 'Do I have to walk the plank?'

I glanced towards the land, knowing I'd have no problem swimming that far.

'If we don't fuck,' said Nick, 'we might as well do something while we're out here. There aren't any fishing rods on board, so I suppose we could go swimming.'

'We could.'

'And you'll just wear a smile?' he asked, with a smile.

'Yes.'

His smile widened.

'If you wear the same,' I added.

He said nothing for several seconds. 'Okay,' he agreed.

'Okay,' I echoed – and I took off my T-shirt.

Nick's eyes instantly focused on my bare boobs. My hair had grown much longer since last year, but it still wasn't long enough to cover my tits. I raised my arms, running my fingers through my hair, and the only reason I did it was so that my breasts would rise up. Under Nick's gaze, my nipples began to harden.

'Your turn,' I told Nick.

He removed the money-belt. 'Now yours,' he said.

Standing up, I unclipped the front of my shorts, hooked my thumbs into the sides, and pushed them down. But I was still wearing the belt, and the money-pouch was large enough to cover my crotch. I stood with my hands on my hips, looking at him.

'Your turn again,' I said, directing my eyes towards his swimsuit and what it contained. I couldn't help noticing that the bulge at the front was far more prominent. 'Don't be shy.'

'I'm not shy.'

'Don't be embarrassed.'

149

'I'm not embarrassed.'

'Then get 'em off.'

He shed his trunks. Removed from its confinement, his cock immediately became horizontal, pointing towards me. I studied his prick and nodded my approval. Then I let the money-pouch fall. As I stood totally nude in front of Nick, his knob continued its ascent towards the vertical – which was his indication of approval.

'Are you sure you don't want to fuck?' he asked.

I was tempted to answer by diving overboard, but I didn't trust Nick. Once I was in the water, I'd be at his mercy. Having spurned his blatant advances, he might decide to keep my clothes and make me wade ashore naked – while it was still daylight, the beach full of people.

I smiled and stepped towards him.

The boat had been rocking from side to side with the rhythm of the waves, and it swayed even more as I approached him. He reached out his right hand to support me, and I stretched out my arm. Then the boat dipped, I leaned aside, grabbed his arm, pulled hard.

'No,' I answered.

I released his arm, and Nick toppled overboard, plunging headlong into the ocean and vanishing from sight. I stared down into the water, and I waited for him to surface – and waited. At first, I wasn't too concerned. But half a minute passed and I was wondering if I was going to have to dive in and rescue him, when the boat suddenly dipped. I spun around. Nick had silently come up on the other side of the dinghy, and he was reaching out towards my legs, hoping to drag me into the water with him.

I avoided his lunge by leaping over the other side and into the sea.

Nick was an excellent swimmer, he could have caught me had he wished, but it seemed he didn't want to. It was evident that he preferred not to chase girls, that he expected them to surrender. I made sure I kept close to the boat, in case he decided to leave without me. We swam for several minutes, saying nothing, almost ignoring each other. When he finally hauled himself over the stern, I made sure that I was close by. He reached down and took one of my hands, helping me on board.

We stood opposite each other, water dripping from our naked bodies, his right hand still clasping mine. I expected him to put his arms around my waist, to pull me close in a passionate embrace, to kiss the salt water away from my lips.

But he released my hand, moved away, and said: 'You want an ice cream?'

That wasn't what I wanted, but I said: 'How much?'

He laughed. 'Cheaper than you sell them. Free, in fact. I'll get the money from my next customers.'

'Okay,' I agreed.

I still hadn't sampled any of the products that I sold, and now was as good a time as any. We sat facing each other; Nick on the decking and me on the seat in the prow. My nipples were still hard, but Nick's cock was no longer erect. Both of these were our physical reactions to having been in the cold ocean. Now that he was out of the sea, there should have been another anatomical change in Nick's physiology. I waited for the natural male response to being with a naked girl – and waited, and waited.

He was being deliberately casual, and I wasn't used to this. Nick had had an erection earlier, so why was his prick now hanging limp between his legs? It was almost an insult. Didn't he fancy me? I knew he did.

'What would you like?' he asked, as he opened the cool box. 'A drink? A frostie? An ice?'

'A scooped cone,' I said. 'And no small measures.'

He filled the cone with vanilla ice cream, and passed it to me. Then he scooped out another serving for himself. I licked at mine, and tried not to gaze at his flaccid cock.

Perhaps this was his other technique. I'd refused him before, and now he was demonstrating that his bodily lusts were subservient to his mental powers. He probably wanted me to turn him on. That was fine by me, because it was also what I wanted.

Nick looked so cool and relaxed, leaning back against the seat at the stern. But I decided to accept the challenge to resurrect his knob.

I also leaned back, arching my spine over the bows so that my breasts pointed upwards as I gazed at the sky. My hips slid forward along the seat, and I spread my legs as if to support my weight, but really to position my open crotch directly in Nick's line of vision. I opened my mouth wide as I lowered the cone towards my lips, thrusting out my tongue to lap at the ice cream. I stroked my free hand over my torso, as if wiping away drops of water from my stomach and ribs, my boobs and nipples. Maybe my methods weren't very subtle . . .

'How do you like the job?' he asked.

I watched him from the corner of my eye, as he watched me from the corner of his eye. Because of the angle at which I was stretched out, I couldn't quite see his dick.

'It's great,' I answered. 'You were right. Whenever I smile and stick out my tits, I make more money.' As I spoke, I smiled and leaned back further, and my tits stuck out even more.

'Putting up the prices probably helps,' said Nick.

I laughed. 'Probably. But that's an extra charge, an entertainment tax. What I should do, I suppose, is experiment by wearing different clothes. Would I sell more if I wore less?'

'You could hardly wear less.'

'But would a bikini top be better than a T-shirt? If I

152

wear a loose T-shirt, it falls open at the front when I lean forward. Like this.'

To demonstrate, I leaned forward, letting Nick see my boobs from a different angle. And I saw that his penis was at a different angle, having become half-erect.

'I didn't realize at first,' I continued, as I glanced down at my breasts, 'but if they get close enough, there's quite a good view. And to get close enough, they have to buy an ice cream. I'm talking about the guys, of course. I do seem to attract a lot of male customers. But I don't think they can see my nipples, can they?'

I stroked my nipples with the fingers of my free hand, and they became even more erect at my touch. Meanwhile, Nick was becoming even more erect as I spoke.

'Not as well as I can,' he replied, no longer pretending not to watch.

'But sometimes the front of my T-shirt brushes across the lid of the cooler, and the fabric gets wet with condensation. You know how cold it is, and so my nipples become hard and the T-shirt becomes almost transparent.'

'You should give lectures in marketing, you know. And I bet your customers never even count their change.'

'I like to give value for money,' I said, taking another lick at my ice cream. I wasn't swallowing any of it; instead I was using my tongue to create a phallic sculpture.

By now, Nick's cock was also as vertical – and I had created both erections. I noticed that he had been working on his own ice cream. The scoop had been spherical, but he had produced a nipple right in the centre. I watched as he ran his tongue around it, and he watched as my tongue flickered up the penile length I had produced.

153

I wondered how much longer he could carry on with the pretence of ignoring my nubile nude body. He could hardly have failed to notice that my labia had become swollen and moist, and my clitoris must have been clearly visible to him.

And I wondered how much longer I could ignore his inviting prick. It was totally erect by now, the glans having grown free of the foreskin.

Nick was very handsome, and his cock was equally good-looking. Although Bruce and I seemed to have gone through every sexual variation inside his car, there was one thing which I hadn't yet done: I hadn't sucked cock.

Nick's shaft looked so tempting and tasty, but having caused it to rise I tried not to submit to its potent attraction. I was determined that he would be the one to make the next move. Until then, I made do with licking at my ice cream. Nick was also licking at his, his tongue still teasing the icy white nipple. I moved my ice cream away from my mouth, and I stroked it across each of my nipples. This caused me to shiver twice, with delight as well as with cold. Drops of thick white cream hung from each of my nipples, but Nick still didn't take the hint.

'When I first saw you,' he said, 'I didn't think you'd stick the job. It's not as easy as it seems. You weren't the first to try it this year, and the others all gave up after what happened the first day. But I'm glad you stuck with it.'

'I'm glad, too,' I said. Then I looked at him, a trace of suspicion beginning to cloud my mind. I remembered what had happened on my first day, when I earned nothing, and I asked: 'What do you know about the first day?'

'It happened to me my first day, years ago.'

'What happened?'

Nick shrugged. 'It's like an initiation ceremony, to make sure you're tough enough for the job.'

'What is?'

I remembered the trouble I'd had with my first customers, the foreign students and the holidaymakers; but I realized that Nick wasn't talking about this. He must have been referring to what was loaded into my trike, that there had been fewer supplies than I believed. I thought it had been the kiosk owner trying to cheat me. It hadn't – it was Nick!

'You bastard!' I said. 'You cheated me! You fucking robbed me!'

He shrugged. 'It's traditional. It happened to me, it happened to you. There was no harm done. I'm sure you've earned extra to make up for it. It was a joke. There's no need to get upset.'

'A joke, you say, a joke! Some fucking joke! You see me laughing?'

'Calm down, calm down.'

'That's not a joke – this is a joke!'

With that I upturned my ice cream and thrust it onto Nick's hard-on, twisting and pushing it down as far as it would go.

'Ahhhhhh . . . !'

He yelled out as the cone slid over his cock, the cream oozing down his shaft. And I laughed out loud.

He glanced down, and I expected him to release his prick from its icy prison. Instead, he left it there, and he lunged forward, shoving his own ice cream towards my chest. He caught me between my boobs, and I screamed as my flesh was instantly frozen. He let go, and his cone remained stuck against my skin.

'That's your kind of joke, is it?' he said, laughing.

He reached into the cooler box, pulled out a can of cola, shook it, aimed it towards me, and ripped back the tab. I was sprayed with a fountain of icy liquid. It went all over my face, my hair, my tits. His ice cream fell into my lap, smearing my pubic hairs with streaks of white. It looked very much like spunk.

I shouted out in shock, and then I dived towards

155

him, trying to reach the cooler box, hunting for another weapon I could use against him. He slammed the lid shut before I made it, but in doing so he slipped onto his back and slid further down the decking. I put my knee on his chest, holding him down, and laughed as I gazed at his dick with the cone still stuck to it.

And I couldn't resist any longer . . .

I knelt above him, taking the cone and his cock in one hand. Nick was watching, and I bared my teeth as I opened my mouth – and bit down hard. He squirmed and tried to escape, but he was too late. My teeth went straight through the end of the cone, biting off the tip. Ice cream squirted all over my mouth, as if he had already ejaculated a spectacular volcano of semen. I raised my face so that he could see, and I licked at my lips, swallowing every drop. He grinned, raising his head so that he could watch properly as I went down on him again.

My mouth opened wide, and I drew the cone between my teeth, tearing at it with my teeth in my eagerness to find his prick. His glans appeared, covered with ice cream. I licked it all away, turning white to purple, and I kept on licking at the domed flesh. It was cold at first, but soon became warm at the touch of my tender tongue. I sucked it into my mouth, blew it out again, before circling my lips around the ridge beneath the glans, while my tongue probed the slit at the very tip. I closed my eyes, no longer needing to see what I was doing, then drew the shaft deeper within, deeper and deeper, before releasing the throbbing flesh, lapping it clean with my tongue and chewing away the last remains of the cone. My mouth glided adoringly from the very apex down to the base of the shaft, sucking at the melted ice cream which had pooled into the pubic hairs, teasing the hairs between my teeth. Then lower, even lower, my tongue flicking in and out to savour the drops which had dripped down onto the testicles. I fed the balls between my teeth, first one, then the other, then both together, feeling them tighten within my mouth. Releasing them, I slowly worked my way back up the shaft, which was now wet with my saliva, before engulfing the helmet between my lips once more, rubbing it all around my mouth, between my teeth and gums, over the inside of my cheeks, across my tongue, tasting the first exquisite drop of spunk as it oozed from its tip. While my lips slid up and down its wondrous length, my lips caressed the firm male flesh from outside and my tongue stroked the shaft from within.

Nick had done nothing but lie there and accept my devoted worship, but now I felt his hands on the side of my face, stroking my cheeks. Then I realized that he was trying to raise my head. He was warning me that he was about to come.

But that was what I wanted. This was no longer his penis, it was mine. I had created his erection, I had caused his impending orgasm. That was also mine, and I wanted it and needed it. I wanted him to climax between my lips, to feel his spunk splatter inside my mouth, to taste his come on my tongue, to swallow every last precious drop down my throat.

As I devoured Nick's cock, trying to feed as much of his virile flesh into my mouth as I could, for him to become part of me, I felt a familiar heat rapidly developing within myself.

I shook my head to make Nick release me, and his knob wobbled wetly between my lips. A second later, I felt his cock start to tremble, but I kept on slurping and sucking, licking and lapping.

Then there was a sudden strong vibration within Nick's penis, and my mouth was filled with the first burst of semen. I gasped with pleasure at the unique sensation. Another eruption, and more sperm shot into my mouth, followed by more and yet more. I kept on sucking and sucking, as if there was an inexhaustible supply. Even when the throbbing flesh between my lips became still, I continued with my oral affections, hoping there would be more delicious drops for me to taste. But then I felt the shaft start to lose its rigidity, and reluctantly I let it slide free.

I opened my eyes and sat up. Nick was leaning back, supporting his head with his hands. I opened my mouth and showed him my tongue. Nick stared as I thrust it out as far as possible. It was thick with creamy spunk; I'd saved every drop. Then I curled my tongue, sucked his gift back into my mouth, and I swallowed.

'Not bad, are they?' I said, licking my lips. 'No wonder people buy them.'

He laughed out loud, then reached towards the cooler box.

'Now it's your turn,' he said. 'How about one of those? Strawberry, I think. It's a lovely pink colour.'

I shook my head. 'No.'

'Yes.'

I started to back away, but Nick grabbed my ankle – and also there was nowhere to go.

In his other hand he held the frostie. It was a long stick of flavoured ice, oval in cross-section. He ripped at the wrapper with his teeth and began to lick it, running his tongue over the rounded end. He pulled at my foot, sliding me closer and closer towards him.

'Don't!' I warned.

'Why not? These are very nice.'

'Don't you dare!'

I tried to close my legs, but couldn't because he was kneeling between them.

'You'll like it, I promise. If you don't, you can have a refund.'

I felt very nervous but equally excited, and now I laughed, forcing myself to relax. Nick licked the end of the ice again.

'Try it,' he said, holding it towards my mouth.

'No.'

'How about here?'

He moved his hand lower, and rubbed the tip of the frostie across each of my nipples, where there were still traces of ice cream. I shuddered at the delightful torture. He leaned over me and drew my right nipple into his mouth, warming it with his tongue; then he did the same to my left one.

He touched the ice to my sternum, and I shivered as he slid it down my torso, leaving a trail of melted pink juice. I was supporting myself on my elbows, and I watched as the ice stick moved lower and lower, until it reached my pubis, which was still sticky with ice cream. Nick stopped for a moment, then he stroked the ice all over my pubic mound, from side to side, up and down, rubbing and rubbing until my hairs were soaking wet. That wasn't the only part of me which was wet, and I shivered again, my whole body quaking in anticipation. The pink ice moved lower, lower, down towards my vulva.

Nick paused, and his eyes met mine. I didn't tell him to stop.

The ice glided over my clitoris, and I cried out. I'd expected it to be cold, but that wasn't what I felt. The heat which had earlier begun to build up far within me suddenly flared again. I could wait no more. I wanted Nick to hurry, and I spread my legs wide in invitation. The frozen tip slipped between my labia, and I moaned with pleasure. I thrust my hips upwards, sliding my vaginal lips across the icy phallus, taking it even deeper into my cunt.

Nick slid the frostie out slightly, then back in, twisting it around and around between my labia, changing the angle so that it also stroked across my quivering clit.

In a matter of seconds I came, my whole body writhing in absolute ecstasy, and I shrieked in total triumph as I climaxed.

'Not so loud,' said Nick. 'They'll hear you on shore and think it's a distress call.'

I was too exhausted to say anything. All I could do was sink down into the bottom of the boat. Even before I could start to descend from the peak which I had reached, I felt something else touch my twat.

Nick was thirstily drinking the melted ice from my hot cunt . . .

As his lips and tongue raised me towards another amazing orgasm, I wondered what it would be like to kiss him.

Chapter Eleven

It turned out that Nick was as good at kissing as he was at licking cunt. We were to do a lot of kissing after that, plus everything else. What we did on our first voyage may not technically have admitted us to the mile-out club, but the next time we went out in the dinghy we definitely met the full qualifications.

Fucking on board a small boat was even more difficult than it had been in Bruce's car, but at least it was always warm and we could roll overboard into the sea afterwards in order to cool down. We even tried fucking *in* the sea, which usually meant that one of us half drowned, whoever happened to be underneath at the time. It turned out to be a lot easier screwing in the shallows, where we could either touch the sand with our toes or else lie across the beach while the breakers pounded over naked writhing bodies.

We always did the latter at night, of course, rolling over and over together at the water's edge. But it was always very erotic to be standing waist-deep in the ocean, screwing away whilst surrounded by swimmers and windsurfers and boats. They were all amusing themselves in the sea, but I was convinced that our aquatic pastimes were far more fun.

Because I was spending so much time with Nick, and we fucked at least once or twice every day, it meant I had fewer hours to sell ice creams. The only way to make up for this drop in income was to take another job, a second job. As soon as I locked up my icemobile for the night, I went off to work again, this time serving drinks in one of the seafront bars. Once again, how much I earned was up to me. There was a basic wage this time, but it was very low. I could

161

make far more in tips – and there was always plenty to drink.

Nick wasn't able to borrow his friend's boat every day, which was just as well because, despite the cooler, some of my supplies tended to melt by the time we returned to shore – which meant I lost money every time we boarded the boat. But it was worth it . . .

Whenever we set sail, it was always a new voyage of sexual discovery. And if we couldn't fuck out to sea, we'd fuck on the beach when the bar closed.

I was going to bed very late, getting up very early, working every day and every night of the week, selling ice creams while it was light, selling drinks when it was dark, and fucking Nick at every opportunity. Yet I seldom felt tired. I seemed to thrive on all the work and all the screwing. I had a wonderful summer, and there was even time to go swimming and to improve my suntan. Most of the improvement was from all the hours we spent in the boat, because I was always naked, and the sea reflected and magnified the intensity of the sun's rays.

If we didn't go out in the boat, we'd meet up for an hour or two in the early afternoon to swim and laze on the sand. We would rendezvous near the pier, which was always the busiest part of the beach. I would have preferred to meet elsewhere, but this was Nick's territory, the area where he sold his frozen wares. More often than not, I would have to swim alone, because Nick had to stay with his cooler, unless he found a friend to look after the tray. Otherwise, he was never off-duty. Even if he was lying half-asleep on the sand, people would approach him to buy something.

I could understand why he had chosen this in preference to pedalling the trike. He didn't have to go looking for customers: they came to him. Although I knew he didn't earn as much as I did, even after he'd increased his prices, the work was a lot easier.

Perhaps next year I'd take over this job, I thought. I'd much rather have stayed on the beach all the time. Nick wouldn't want to sell ices any more, because he'd have left college by then. But I didn't know where I'd be next year, or what I'd be doing. The more I considered the matter, the more I hoped I wouldn't be here, wouldn't be selling ice creams and drinks to tourists. I wanted to be somewhere else, a place where *I* could be a tourist.

The beaches by the pier, I gradually realized, were more than merely a place of work for Nick. They offered another attraction for him and just about every other male in town. This was what Helen had mentioned to me last year: it was where the foreign students came to sunbathe topless.

They didn't seem to work many hours at the language schools. Whether it was morning or afternoon, there were always some of them on the beach, stripped down to their bikini briefs. The men who worked in the nearby offices and shops would line the promenade at lunchtime, leaning on the railings. Most would pretend that they weren't really watching the free striptease show. Others were less subtle and would bring binoculars or cameras with telephoto lenses. It would have been a great patch for selling ice creams, except that the guy who owned the kiosk wouldn't allow me to operate within a hundred yards of the pier; that part of the promenade was his territory.

Not all the foreign students would bare their breasts, of course. And there would never be just one of them who was stripped to the waist; it seemed that they could only expose themselves in company. Sometimes there were a score of half-naked girls on the beach, sometimes only a quarter that many. But there always appeared to be one who was getting dressed to go back to her academy, and another would arrive and undress to take her place. Nick's job gave him the perfect opportunity to wander amongst them, trying to sell ices.

'Don't you get bored?' I asked him.

We were side by side, sitting on the sand and leaning against one of the breakwaters. As usual, I was wearing shorts and a T-shirt, although over the summer my outfit had become more and more abbreviated. The T-shirt was little more than a vest, sleeveless and with a plunging neckline at both the front and back; and my shorts were exactly that – very short, with a slit up each side almost to the waistband.

Despite this, Nick was paying far more attention to the slim brunette ten yards away. Like me, she was also wearing a pair of shorts – but only a pair of shorts. She was, however, lying prone on the sand, tanning her back.

'Bored with what?' he asked, but he smiled.

He knew exactly what I was referring to. He was wearing his usual outfit of swimming trunks, and he glanced at me before nodding to another girl lying fifteen yards away. Neither was she wearing a bra, but she was supine, baring her breasts to the sun – and to everyone else who was watching.

'I could be looking at her,' he said.

'At her what? Her tits, you mean? So why aren't you? Because you've already seen them?'

'No, hers aren't very interesting. She's lying flat, you can't really see anything. Her nipples aren't even erect.' He looked away and directed his gaze at the brunette again.

'You can see even less of her,' I said. 'Only her bare back.'

'I know, but when she turns over, her tits will come into view – and they'll be the proper shape.'

'Tit-shaped tits, huh? But she might not turn over. Or if she does, she might cover herself first.'

164

'Exactly! She *might* roll over. She *might* show her tits, even for only a moment while she stretches out her arm. But that's what makes her worth watching.'

I nodded, beginning to understand. 'So you don't really want to see bare tits, you just want to dream about seeing them?'

'I do want to see them. But I want them to do something, not just lie there.'

'See them do what?'

'I want the girl to move, to sit up, to stand up, to walk around. Better still, to run and jump along the beach. I want to see tits that jiggle.'

'You see many topless girls skipping along the beach, doing handstands and cartwheels?'

'If only,' Nick sighed. 'Most of them just lie there, facing up or facing down. Sometimes they might sit up, but that's all. If only one of them would go swimming topless.' He glanced at me, glanced at my boobs.

I pretended not to notice, but I raised my hands high above my head and then let them drop, which caused my breasts to rise and fall, swaying up and down for a moment. About twenty-five yards away, there was a girl sitting up reading a book, and all she was wearing was a monokini.

'If you've seen two, haven't you seen them all?' I asked.

'No, they're all different. Every girl is different, and every girl's breasts are different; different shapes, different sizes.'

'Like cocks, I suppose.'

'I wouldn't know.'

'But I would.'

He looked at me for a moment, then continued to survey the beach. 'Listen: just because I admire a girl's tits, it doesn't mean I want to fuck her.'

'Yes it does.'

'Well . . . yes, maybe it does.'

He ducked aside as I aimed a playful punch at his head, and he grinned.

'Don't pretend,' he continued. 'I've seen you looking at other girls' tits. But it doesn't mean you want to fuck them.'

'It might.'

'What?' He stared at me again and was silent for a few seconds, then shook his head. 'No, you're like me, you're simply taking an aesthetic interest in a work of art. A nice pair of tits is one of the great wonders of nature.'

'Do I have a nice pair of tits?'

'You've got a great pair! Why don't you take your T-shirt off?'

'Isn't it more exciting for you if I *don't* – because then I *might* . . . ?'

He laughed.

'Anyway,' I said, 'you've seen my boobs. But do you want everyone else to see them?'

'Yeah, I do. I'm proud of you. I'm proud of your tits.'

'And you want to sit next to me, so everyone can think: *Look at that lucky bastard with the topless girl.*'

'Exactly. They can look, but they can't touch. Where's the harm in it? I'm looking at these girls. They don't mind. So why should you mind anyone else looking at you?'

'I don't.'

'So you'll take off your T-shirt?'

'No,' I said.

'Why not?'

Because I was having more fun teasing Nick by not taking it off, but I said: 'I'll take it off if you take off your trunks.'

'You're kidding!'

I was, but I shook my head. 'What's the difference?'

'You know what the difference is. Tits are beautiful, but cocks are ugly.'

166

'You don't think yours is ugly, do you?'

'Do you?'

'Yes!'

'But that's something completely different. It's like you showing your twat. Not even that, because what would you reveal if you dropped your shorts? Only your pubic hairs, and they cover your cunt. Women look great naked, men look stupid.'

'Definitely,' I agreed.

'You know what I mean. What's a bit of hair? Hair on your head, hair between your legs, so what? But a guy without his pants – you can see *everything*.'

'I know.' I sighed wistfully.

'When you put your swimsuit on,' Nick continued, 'you have to go through such contortions in case you expose a square inch of tit. It would be much easier if you didn't bother, if you went swimming in your bikini pants.'

'Or even without them.'

'Yeah.'

'Shut up and give me a cola.'

'It'll cost you.'

I flipped up the hem of my T-shirt, baring my boobs for a split second.

'Will that pay for a can?' I asked.

He laughed and opened his tray, passing me the drink and taking one for himself. I noticed him looking past me, and I turned my head. A slender redhead in an expensive woollen skirt and matching jacket was walking across the sand, carrying her high-heeled shoes in one hand. Although she wasn't wearing the regular uniform of short skirt and T-shirt, the logo on her holdall labelled her as one of the language students. She was probably my age, and she must have been roasting inside her outfit. I wondered if she was going to take it off – and I realized that was exactly what Nick must have been thinking. I glanced at him for a moment.

'Whenever a guy sees a good-looking girl,' he told me, as he watched the redhead, 'you can't help undressing her with your eyes, wondering what she's like under her clothes.' He shrugged. 'It's just a fantasy.'

The girl halted about fifteen yards away, joining two more of the foreign students, both of whom were wearing bikinis. The three girls began speaking to each other. The redhead stood with her back to us as she dropped her shoes on the beach, took out a towel from the bag and spread it on the sand. She removed her jacket and slipped one of her hands into the waistband of her skirt, then wiggled her hips from side to side. A few seconds later, her white satin panties slid down her calves. She put them into her bag and pulled out a pair of bright blue bikini pants. Stepping into them, she pulled them all the way up to her hips, which meant that her skirt also rode up her thighs. Then she unfastened the skirt and let it fall.

Although she was facing away from us, I could tell that she was undoing the buttons of her blouse, and she let it slip down over her shoulders. She had a black bra underneath. One of the other girls said something and pointed out to sea, and the redhead began to turn towards the ocean. As she did so, she fingered the centre of her bra. Suddenly the garment came apart; it was one whch fastened at the front. She was facing Nick and I as her breasts came free, and they swayed from side to side.

'And sometimes,' said Nick, 'the fantasy comes true.'

I realized that I had been as fascinated by watching the girl disrobe as he had, and my attention was fully focused on her bare boobs.

'Is that how you imagined her?' I asked.

'Better.'

Although she was slender and slim-hipped, her

168

breasts were quite large. Her rose-coloured nipples were hard, slightly upturned.

Not to be outdone, I peeled off my T-shirt, and my nipples were also erect.

Nick's eyes moved from the redhead's tits to mine, and he smiled. I noticed that the foreign girl was watching me. Then she turned around and sat down with her friends.

'Anything they can do,' I said, 'I can do *better*.'

Nick nodded. 'I'd love to give them a lick.'

'I'm not stopping you,' I said.

'Perhaps later.'

'More than *perhaps*, I hope.' Then I added: 'I've gone this far, I might as well go all the way.'

I slid my thumbs into the sides of my shorts and slowly started to push them down. For a moment, it seemed that Nick was too surprised to stop me. My pubic hairs had begun to show before he grabbed my wrist and hissed: 'Stop it!'

'What's wrong?' I asked.

'You know what's wrong.'

I couldn't say anything else because I started laughing.

'You!' laughed Nick, but then his eyes shifted direction and he was gazing at the redhead's bare back.

'She *might* turn around?' I said.

'Yes, and she *might* rub suntan oil over her tits. Or, even better, one of her friends *might* do it for her.'

'Is this more of the fantasy? You want to see a girl rub oil over her boobs?'

I reached down to my bag. Nick glanced away from the redhead so he could watch my boobs sway as I moved. I pulled out a bottle of suntan oil.

'I'm your dream come true, Nick,' I said. I passed him the bottle. 'Or do you want to rub it into my tits?'

'No, no. Not here, not now.'

'I don't know.' I shook my head. 'You won't suck

my nipples, won't let me take off my shorts, won't stroke my boobs. Here, pour some into each hand.'

I held out my palms and he did as he was told, and I began to massage the oil into my breasts. I remembered having done this last year at Helen's, and now I slowly rubbed the oil over both of my bare breasts. As I did so, I licked at my lips and began to pant, softly at first, then louder and faster. This was for Nick's benefit, but as I continued to smear the oil over my boobs, my nipples became fully dilated and I realized how pleasurable it was. I enjoyed stroking my breasts, and I enjoyed it even more because I was touching myself up in public. I crossed my arms, so that I rubbed my right boob with my left hand, my left with my right.

I reached for the oil and let it drop down onto my tits, and I said: 'I'd like to rub this all over your prick, up and down, up and down, smear it all over the head of your cock and watch the drips roll down the shaft and onto your balls. Up and down, up and down, wanking you harder and harder.'

As I spoke, Nick shifted uneasily. His hands had been by his sides, but now he clasped them over his lap. I could make out the outline of his cock as it began to expand and stiffen within his trunks.

'Harder and harder,' I repeated, while I continued massaging my breasts. 'Don't you just wish we could fuck right here?'

'We will,' promised Nick. 'Tonight. Right here.'

We did.

And it was great.

It was always great.

Neither of us knew it, but that was to be our last fuck together.

I'd met Nick less than two months ago, and he had become such an important part of my life that it seemed impossible I hadn't known him forever.

Instead of growing bored with him, the opposite became true. Although we never really did anything different from day to day, every dawn was like a new beginning. There was always something fresh to learn, another experience to be shared. The more I knew Nick, the more fun I had with him.

We always had a fucking good time. Literally.

The highlight of my day was when I was with him, and not only when we were screwing in the surf or sucking each other off in the dinghy. Even if we were only side by side, not even touching, not saying a word, I was happy.

I suppose I was in love . . .

The next morning a tourist coach happened to stop near where I was selling, and I rode on a few yards to see if I could find a few customers. I found more than a few, because the air-conditioning had broken down and everyone on board was boiling hot. The day-trippers almost cleaned me out of stock, and so it was much earlier than usual when I pedalled back towards the pier for more supplies.

This usually happened halfway through the day, although the time could vary by as much as an hour. If it was getting too late, and I hadn't sold enough, I wouldn't wait any longer. When I took a break would also depend on whether we were going out in the boat or not; or the tide would be a factor if I'd be swiming from the beach.

Because I'd had a good morning and sold a lot, I thought I'd stop early and surprise Nick. But it was me who got the surprise.

I'd watched him before without him knowing, admiring his supple body as he strolled across the beach, selling ices and drinks. He didn't even need to walk around, because just as often his customers would come up to him.

I couldn't see him as I rode towards the pier, and so I presumed that he must have been further along.

Dismounting, I locked the trike and walked barefoot along the promenade to the next beach. When I looked down, I didn't see him at first, but I saw *her*.

It was the girl from yesterday, the redhead in the expensive suit – and out of the expensive suit. The one with the black front-fastening bra which she'd undone while Nick and I had watched. She was top-less again, this time her bikini pants were bright orange, and this time she was with Nick . . .

For a few seconds I thought that he must have been selling her a drink, which was why they were together. That didn't explain why they were sitting side by side, however, or why they were laughing and talking.

I watched for several minutes, thinking that there must have been some innocent explanation. I kept waiting for Nick to continue selling ice creams, or for the girl to get up and walk away. But they remained together, very close together – and I became more and more angry as I finally accepted that this was no commercial transaction.

I wondered what to do, whether to walk away and pretend I'd seen nothing. That way, I could return an hour later and everything would carry on as always between myself and Nick. But even if I pretended, I couldn't forget what I'd already witnessed.

Or I could have charged down onto the beach, created a scene. That might have allowed me to vent my rage, but would only be a temporary solution. Nick would either say I was completely wrong, I'd misunderstood the situation and he was only helping the student with her irregular verbs, and he'd soon win me around with his smile. After all, what had he been doing? Just sitting next to her, nothing more. It wasn't as if they were fucking.

Not yet. That came next, I knew.

Or else if I suddenly appeared, Nick might choose

her instead of me – and that would be the worst thing of all.

I couldn't pretend I hadn't seen them together. Sitting next to a half-naked redhead was anything but innocent. I didn't intend to share him and his cock with any other girl. It was over between us.

I simply turned and walked away. I returned to my trike, unlocked it, and went and loaded up more supplies from the kiosk.

Although I tried not to think of Nick, it was impossible. Instead, I kept thinking of him even more – imagining him naked with the redhead, screwing her on the beach or licking her clit in the boat.

I sat in the saddle and started riding back along the promenade. A line of men leaned against the railings, all of them gazing down at the topless girls on the beach. This was how it had started with Nick, I remembered. He had seen the redhead yesterday, watched her undressing, and had been lured away by her bare breasts.

I was still seething inside at Nick's treachery, but what could I expect? He was only a poor male, helplessly hypnotized by a nice pair of tits. Instead of evaporating, my anger continued to increase. I had to blow off steam, or else I'd burst. Nick had betrayed me for all the world to see, and I needed to make a similar gesture to demonstrate that we were through – and to get even with him.

I suddenly realized how I could do it.

This wasn't my sales pitch, I was still very near the pier, but I halted and called out: 'Ice creams, drinks, ices!'

It was a great idea, but I didn't know if I had the nerve to do it. Then I thought of the redhead, and I knew that I did.

I peeled off my T-shirt . . .

'Ice creams, drinks, ices!' I called.

One of the men nearest to me glanced around for a

173

moment, then began to look away before he became aware of what he had seen: my bare boobs. He paused, turned around and stared at me.

'Ice creams, drinks, ices!'

I pressed down on the pedals and the trike started to move away. The man realized there was only one way he could keep me there, and he stepped towards me, reaching into his pocket for his money.

'Yes?' I said, braking. 'What would you like?'

He looked at my tits, looked at my face, looked at my tits again. He'd take anything, I realized.

I opened the cooler box, reached in, gave him a can of cola. There hadn't been time to replace my price stickers, but I charged him double what I usually did. He didn't seem to notice.

By then, I had another customer, then another and another and another. I never sold so much so fast – and for so much . . .

There were plenty of topless girls down on the beach, but the men who had been watching the half-naked foreign students could get within a yard of my bare boobs. And by buying an ice cream from me, they had a perfect excuse for doing so.

As well as being closer to them, my tits *moved*. They bounced up and down as I leaned over the cooler box, they jiggled from side to side when I turned to hand out a frostie. Being the centre of so much attention, my nipples soon dilated, while my breasts became speckled with drops of ice cream which melted and dripped down my naked flesh.

Having so many men around me was great, and I really enjoyed myself. I kept expecting someone to come along and tell me to cover myself up, but no one did. My customers and everyone else must have appreciated the view.

In a matter of minutes, I'd sold almost everything the icemobile carried, and I hadn't ridden anywhere. I could have done this in the kiosk, I realized, and made a fortune. That wasn't my intention. My decision to strip off had been a crazy impulse. I had no intention of continuing as a topless salesgirl, even if I was allowed to.

But after this, nothing would be the same. I couldn't cover my tits and continue riding up and down the promenade selling ice creams. Just as it was all over between me and Nick, I decided that I was finished with the job. As soon as the box was empty, that would be the end.

'Hey!'

I turned at the sound of the voice and saw the photographer three yards away. He was Phil of Phil's Photos, who was always on the promenade trying to persuade tourists to have their picture taken.

'What are you doing?' I asked.

'Taking your photo, of course.' As if to prove it, I heard his camera click. 'Is that okay by you?'

'Does it make any difference?'

He laughed. 'No.' He took some more shots.

I looked at the guys standing nearby, all of whom were watching me. I glanced at Phil, shrugged, and my boobs jiggled.

'Go ahead,' I told him.

I arched my back so that my bare breasts thrust out even more; and I stuck out my tongue, fellating the cone which I held. Ice cream dripped from my lips and down the side of my mouth, and I heard the camera go *click click click*.

Although I knew this was the end of my temporary job, I was totally unaware that it was also the start of my true career.

Chapter Twelve

I was suddenly famous, or notorious, and became something of a local celebrity. Although I'd probably bared my boobs for no more than ten minutes, that was plenty of time for Phil and his camera – and photos are forever.

My picture appeared on the front page of the local paper the next day, although it was one taken at such an angle that my nipples were discreetly covered by an arm as I held out a frostie. The editor of the newspaper wrote a jokey article about how I could become a tourist attraction and that I should appear on the cover of the town's next holiday brochure.

Phil also managed to sell a photo of me to one of the city papers; and there was no modesty when that picture was published. My bare breasts were in full view as I sat on the trike and offered an ice cream to one of my admiring customers.

By way of thanks, Phil took me for an expensive meal. At first I refused to go out with him, but I realized that he had been paid for the photograph and this was the only reward I'd ever get. I suspected that there was more to his invitation than him expressing his gratitude. If a man took a girl to a restaurant, he usually had only one idea in mind: to get her out of her clothes.

I was right, because that was also Phil's intention; but I was only half-right, because he claimed he wanted to do this for professional reasons. He hoped to take a series of nude photographs of me – although he'd probably have had more success if he just wanted to fuck me.

A week had gone by since I'd split up with Nick. If

I hadn't stripped off my T-shirt, and if I hadn't given up the job, then maybe I wouldn't have kept to my resolution of breaking up. Things would have continued as before, and we'd have kept on fucking as before. But I had no regrets about leaving Nick or about my topless selling technique.

Photographic evidence of the latter had inevitably caused some trouble at home, which secretly pleased me. If my parents disapproved of something, that was good enough reason for me doing it.

But there weren't enough other reasons for me to agree to Phil's suggestion that I should pose nude for him. Perhaps if I fancied him more, or if I believed that a modelling session would also lead to a good fuck, I might have gone along with it. Instead, I told him 'no' and went off to work.

Although I'd given up one job, I still had the other, and I continued working in the bar every night. There were many similar establishments in town, and the boss was always looking for ways to increase trade. Because of my recent fame, he had offered to double my pay if I'd work topless. I didn't want to do that, partly because it was too obvious. Instead, inspired by my conversation with Nick on the subject of bare-breasted sunbathers, I came up with a more subtle idea.

The girls who served drinks in the bar all wore the same black velvet uniform of ankle boots, shorts, vest. This was meant to look nautical, being decorated with gold braid and topped off by a sailor's peaked cap. The vest was like a waistcoat, with brass buttons sewn down the front. Although the buttons didn't unfasten, there was a deep V-neck which revealed plenty of cleavage. I suggested that the vests should be replaced by waistcoats which really did unfasten at the front – and which remained unfastened.

This meant that whenever we turned or bent down or raised our arms, the front of the waistcoat *might*

177

open wide enough to bare one of the wearer's boobs. (Compared to the boss's suggestion, it *was* subtle . . .)

I wouldn't have worn such a garment if none of the others did, but for a suitable financial incentive all the girls who worked there agreed to dress the same. The lights were kept quite low in the bar, and also how much tit we exposed depended on us. We all became adept at almost revealing our nipples. Although it had only been operating for three nights, everyone seemed happy with the arrangement. More men came to the place, which pleased the boss; the customers were pleased with what they saw or thought they *might* see; and the girls were pleased with the pay increase.

Changing into my velvet uniform, I began work. Having already consumed several glasses of wine during my meal, I was in total harmony with the theme of the bar: I was floating. I worked on automatic pilot, serving drinks, collecting glasses, wiping tables, and the hours quickly went by.

I was behind the bar when I became aware that I was under observation. This wasn't at all unusual. It would have been very strange if no one was looking at me. There were always eyes on me whatever I did, watching for the gap at the front of my waistcoat to become even wider, hoping that my bare boobs would be fully exposed. I continued working, not taking much notice, but I could still sense the same steady gaze surveying my body. When I glanced in that direction, however, I noticed that it was a woman who was studying me.

Although I was used to men's lustful stares, and being undressed by male eyes, it felt odd to have a woman watching me in exactly the same manner. She was about thirty years old, very attractive, with shoulder-length ash-blonde hair. One of the other girls must have served her, because there was a drink on the bar in front of her. She didn't look away even when she noticed that I was aware of her. All she did

178

was raise her drink to her lips and continue her blatant appraisal of my body.

She was on her own, but not for long. A tall man sauntered over and leaned against the bar by her side. She ignored him and kept watching me. I didn't hear the words, but I knew he must have asked her if she wanted another drink. Still without looking at the man, she beckoned to him with her index finger. He leaned towards her, and she kept gesturing for him to come closer. She turned her head and whispered in his ear, but her eyes were still on me.

The man suddenly stood up straight and backed away, staring at the woman in total astonishment. She took another drink and ignored him as he walked away.

'That must be a great brush-off line,' I said to her.

'It is,' she agreed, and she smiled. 'But I'm sure you're too young and innocent to understand.'

'I am!' I laughed.

She drained her glass and slid it towards me. 'Another vodka and tonic.'

I reached for another glass, added ice and a slice of lemon, turned, and felt her eyes still on me as I lifted the glass towards the optic. I could easily have raised my arm so that my waistcoat hardly moved, but I didn't. The full curve of my right breast came into view as I filled the glass. I'd done this many times before, teasing the male customers.

There were also many men whose eyes must have been focused on my bare female flesh at that very second, but they meant nothing. I became aware that I was deliberately baring my boob so that it could be seen by a woman; and I was doing it because that was exactly what she wished.

It was also what I wanted, I realized, or I wouldn't have exposed myself. For a woman to be gazing at me in such a way, and for me to be enjoying her blatant

179

stare, gave me a very strange feeling. I felt my nipples begin to dilate.

The woman nodded her thanks for the drink and said: 'One for yourself?'

As always, I'd been offered several drinks that night; I'd accepted the money but only drunk glasses of fruit juice. I glanced up at the clock, making sure that my waistcoat came apart as I twisted around. The place wasn't open much longer. If I wanted a couple of real drinks, it was time to start.

'Thanks,' I said, and I fixed another vodka and tonic.

I continued my work, mixing drinks, serving other customers, and the woman was always watching me. My glass was near to her, and I kept returning so that I could sip at my drink. It was evident that she was fascinated by me, and perhaps that was why I was so drawn to her. Two more men approached her, then retreated with the same look of amazed disbelief after she had whispered in their ears. She bought us both another drink, and then it was closing time.

The boss began the long process of getting everyone out of the door, and the blonde at the bar was one of the last few left in the place.

'Where's the action now?' she asked me.

'You're joking,' I said. 'This is it. It's over.'

'But there must be somewhere else in this town. Where do you usually go now?'

'There is somewhere,' I said. 'You can come with me if you want.'

'I want,' she said.

We met outside and finally introduced ourselves. Her name was Angela, and I led her across the road to the promenade. I pointed down to the beach and the sea.

'That's where I go,' I said. 'For a walk, for a paddle, for a swim.'

I hadn't been for a midnight swim for over a week, partly because I didn't want to encounter Nick screwing the redhead on the beach. It was only when Angela had asked me where I went after work that I'd thought of the idea. At first I wasn't sure that I intended to go swimming; I'd led her here simply to prove there was nowhere else to go. But it was a wonderful night, and the sea looked absolutely perfect.

Angela shook her head in bewilderment. 'That's it, is it? It's what you do around here for late night excitement?'

'Yes. You want to go for a swim?' I turned to face her, then added: 'A nude swim?'

She looked me up and down, and slowly she smiled.

'I don't mind being nude,' she said. 'But do I have to swim?'

'You can't have one without the other.'

'Yes, you can.'

Because I'd dressed to go out with Phil and I didn't want to lead him on, I was wearing my usual summer outfit of sandals, shorts and T-shirt. The shorts were baggier than usual, the T-shirt looser and longer than usual. Angela could hardly have been more different, with stiletto heels and fitted skirt, designer jacket and silk blouse. I didn't really think that she would strip off on the beach – although I tried to imagine it . . .

'I'm going swimming,' I told her, and I made my way down the concrete steps towards the beach.

I heard her heels clicking after me, and so I waited. She took her shoes off, I removed my sandals, and we walked across the beach together. We could hear voices in the distance. There were people already in the water near the pier. I realized that I didn't have a towel, but it was a warm night. The sky was very black, speckled with thousands of stars, and the moon was half-full, its soft radiance reflected upon the calm surface of the ocean.

'Are you coming in?' I asked.

'I'll just watch,' said Angela.

181

I thumbed down my shorts and briefs, pulled my T-shirt over my head – and Angela just watched. She surveyed every inch of my body, but there was nothing sexual in her gaze. It was as if I were something in a shop which she was considering; a new outfit which she might buy. She even walked around me, looking me up and down from the rear, and I simply stood there and let her examine me. Finally she was facing me again, and she smiled.

'You're terrific, you know,' she said.

'I know!' I laughed. Then I turned and ran towards the dark water, plunging through the cold waves and diving beneath the surface.

I'd wanted to go swimming, but I'd also wanted to strip off in front of Angela. But as I swam up and down, I wondered what would happen next. From the way that she had been inspecting me, it didn't seem that her plan was to seduce me. Perhaps she had no plan. She was alone in town; that's why she'd gone to the bar in search of company for a while. I wondered if I was reading too much into the situation. I was becoming cold, but I felt nervous about what would happen once I left the water.

But what could happen? Nothing unless I allowed it to. I had nothing to be nervous about, I decided, and I swam back to the beach. If Angela hadn't been there, I would have run up the sand. That was what I did, my breasts bouncing. She was still standing in the same spot, still watching me.

I picked up my shorts and used them to dry my face, then rubbed as much of my torso as I could before the shorts became too wet. I pulled my T-shirt back on. The hem reached down beneath my buttocks, and the garment clung to my damp body, the nipples thrusting against the fabric.

'My hotel's over the road,' said Angela. 'Do you want to come back and get dry?'

'Yes,' I said.

*

'That's the honeymoon suite,' I said, when Angela collected the key.

She glanced at me, obviously wondering how I knew. It was because I'd cleaned it often enough. She was staying in the hotel where I'd worked.

'It was the only room they had left,' she said, as we headed for the lift.

She opened the door and we went inside. 'You want a shower? Or there's a great bath.'

'I know,' I said.

She glanced questioningly at me again, but I wouldn't explain. There was far more that I wanted to know about her, so I should be allowed some mysteries of my own.

I had been carrying my shorts and panties, and I threw them onto a chair, kicked off my sandals and made my way to the bed. It was a huge four-poster, and I reached for the cord which was hidden behind the headboard.

'Watch,' I said, pointing upwards.

What appeared to be the canopy drew back, and a large mirror was revealed on the ceiling directly above the bed. Angela glanced up at the mirror and smiled.

'Have you been here before, by any chance?' she asked.

'Maybe,' I said, and turned away.

I walked towards the bathroom, discarding my T-shirt as I did so. The walls and ceiling were covered with mirrors, and I could see a dozen reflections of myself. I'd always wanted to try the bath. It was absolutely enormous, sunken and round, with whirlpool jets which fountained out of the sides. I turned the hot tap on full, then I glanced into the bedroom. Angela wasn't even watching; she was talking to someone on the telephone, and I felt oddly disappointed.

When the bath was full and the temperature correct, I turned off the taps and climbed in. The bath was almost big enough to float in, and there was an underwater ledge on which to sit. I lay back and relaxed, before sinking below the surface and letting the warm water rinse the salt from my hair.

Surfacing, I saw Angela's high-heeled shoes by the edge of the bath. I looked upwards. She was wearing a pair of stockings and a red suspender belt; her lace bra and briefs were matching red. Through the steam, I could see her image reflected in the mirrors all around the room. She was holding a tray with two fluted glasses, a silver bucket filled with ice – and a bottle of champagne.

'This *is* the honeymoon suite,' she explained with a shrug, and her breasts rose and fell enticingly.

She put down the tray and I watched as she unhooked her bra. Her boobs came free, and her nipples were the same soft pink as my own. She removed her red briefs, and her pubic curls were the same colour as her pale hair. A few seconds later, her shoes, stockings and suspender belt were gone and she joined me in the bath.

Angela sighed and closed her eyes for a moment, then looked at me. We were opposite one another, our nipples just breaking the surface. She smiled, and so did I.

I studied her nude torso as she stood up again and reached for the champagne, drops of water dripping from her perfect breasts. She untwisted the wire from the neck, popped the cork, and caught the first foaming bubbles of champagne in one of the glasses. Filling both glasses, she turned and passed one to me.

'Cheers.'

'Cheers.'

We clinked the glasses together, and I was about to drink, but instead Angela looped her arm around mine, pulling me closer. As we drank, we gazed deep into one another's eyes. Then the champagne was drained, the glasses gone, and suddenly our lips were pressed together, and we kissed.

It was the first time I had ever kissed another woman like this, kissed her as I would a man, my mouth hard against hers, my lips parting, my tongue meeting hers. I felt her breasts against mine, the firmness of her nipples against my soft flesh. Her arms were around my waist, mine were around her back, clutching our bodies tight together; even our legs seemed to be wrapped around each other. We lost our balance and slipped beneath the water, but our lips remained locked together, our tongues caressing. The waters in the bath began to swirl; one of us must have accidentally hit the whirlpool control.

My head broke surface and I opened my eyes, and I could see dozens of nude female couples kissing and embracing all around us. And the way that the warm waters cascaded around us, it felt as if I were in the bath with many other naked women. There were hands all over my body, fondling my breasts and buttocks, stroking my face and thighs; but they could only have been Angela's hands.

All I could do at first was kiss her, but then my own hands began to respond. They reached out to touch the softness of her breasts – and the hardness of her nipples. My heart was thudding, my blood racing through my veins.

Angela pulled away, allowing me to breathe properly for the first time; but I couldn't breathe properly, because my breath was coming in short, fast bursts.

Her head disappeared beneath the surface, and I felt her mouth upon my left nipple, engulfing my sensitive flesh between her lips, licking it with her expert tongue. Then I felt something lightly brush across my pubis. It must have been one of her hands, and I automatically clamped my thighs together. But I could feel a familiar heat beginning to develop deep

185

within, a heat which could not be quenched by the water in which I was immersed.

Then Angela's head appeared and she shook it, spraying drops of water from her face and her hair. She reached for the champagne bottle, tilted it to her lips, drinking, then raised it above my face. I opened my mouth, but most of the bubbling liquid cascaded over my face. She licked at the golden drops, then we kissed again, sucking each other's lips into our mouths, gently nibbling with our teeth, caressing with our tongues. She pulled away and stared at me.

'Let's fuck,' she said.

She climbed from the bath and held out her hand to me. I accepted, and she pulled me up out of the water. Hand in hand, side by side and soaking wet, we made our way into the bedroom. I fell down upon the bed and gazed up into the mirror. It was as if this wasn't happening to me, that I was a voyeur watching through a window as the two sleek nude blondes passionately embraced.

Their bodies were intertwined and they rolled over and over together, laughing, each one of them trying to get on top of the other, stroking and caressing, licking and kissing, fondling and touching, then finally becoming almost still, the only movement the rise and fall of their damp breasts as they breathed in and out.

The playful battle was over, surrender had been given. Both had their arms outstretched above their heads, their long legs spread wide; but the older one lay above the younger, seeming to pin her down. The novice remained motionless, while her more experienced lover kissed her mouth and her throat, then her breasts.

The naked woman slid down and down, her lips moving lower and lower, kissing every inch of tender young flesh, licking the navel before descending even further, then down, over the pubic mound, tugging lightly at the damp curls with her teeth, then further, further.

I kept staring up into the mirror as Angela's sensuous mouth reached the girl's cunt.

But I was the girl and it was my cunt – and I was wet, wet, wetter than I had even been before.

The flames deep within me raged incandescently, building up towards a fiery crescendo.

I gasped as I felt Angela's hot breath upon my vulva.

I trembled in anticipation as her tongue touched my clitoris.

My whole body writhed in absolute ecstasy as she kissed my cunt, her soft mouth pressed against my swollen labia, her tender tongue probing deep, deep and torching the fuse which sparked the ultimate explosion.

And I came and came.

My hands clutched at Angela's head, forcing her face hard against my twat, not wanting her to escape until every last glowing ember within my white hot core had decayed into a blackened cinder.

I lay still but shuddering, totally relaxed but totally aware, and finally Angela raised her head from the valley between my thighs. She sat up, reached between her lips and pulled out a pubic hair, wiped at her mouth with her fingertips, and then sucked her fingers. She leaned down again and licked the sweat from my belly. I stretched out my arms, stroking her hair, pulling her up towards me. We lay side by side in each other's damp embrace, and we kissed softly. I could taste myself upon her lips.

I must have fallen asleep for a minute, because the next thing I knew I was alone. I gazed up at my nude image in the mirror above me, and I smiled contentedly, wondering what was so strange. It was more than having been to bed with a woman that was different, it was the very fact of having been to bed.

This was the first time I'd had sex in a bed, I realized; the first time I'd even had sex indoors.

The softness and comfort was such a luxury, and idly I wondered how it would feel to have a cock inside my cunt under such sybaritic conditions.

Then Angela was back by my side, and I immediately felt guilty for thinking of a man and his prick under such heavenly circumstances. Her tongue had given me as much as any penis had ever done.

The champagne glasses were refilled. I propped myself up on my elbow, took one of the glasses, and we clinked them together and drank again.

'So,' I said, admiring her lithe nude body, 'what brought you here?'

'You did.'

'No, you brought me here, remember? What brought you to town?'

'You did.'

I studied her face, and I knew she was telling the truth; but that didn't mean I understood.

'You're famous,' Angela continued. 'Your picture has been in newspapers and magazines around the world.'

'The *world*?'

'Yes. Your tits are famous in dozens of countries. There are a lot of people who'd like to see you' – she looked me up and down, and she smiled – 'totally naked. People who would buy a magazine because you're inside it. And I happen to be a photographer . . .'

'What?' I sat bolt upright, spilling some of my champagne.

Angela leaned down and licked the drops from my thigh.

'All this is just so you can take some nude pictures of me!'

She raised her head, shaking it in denial. 'That was the original idea. But I've had a lot more fun than I ever thought – and I hope you have, too.' She tilted her head to one side and looked at me.

I stroked my pubic hairs and nodded; I'd had lots of fun.

'I don't do this with all my models, you know,' she said. 'But I'd like to!'

I moved my hand from my pubes to hers and gave them a gentle tug.

'I began my career as a model,' Angela continued, watching my fingers, 'and now I'm on the other side of the lens.' She nodded towards her luggage in the corner. 'That's some of my equipment over there.'

'You want to take nude pictures of me? Now?'

She shook her head again, and she smiled again. 'Not now. Maybe later. It's all up to you.'

As she spoke, I sipped at my champagne and continued stroking her pubic hairs. She wriggled her hips and sighed, and my fingers moved lower.

'I was given the assignment of locating you and asking if you wanted to do it. You're hot right now –'

'Not as hot as I was!' I said, although touching her up was beginning to warm me again.

' – because of the topless ice cream selling, but I've been in the business long enough to know you could make a good living out of it.'

'Out of spreading my legs and showing my cunt?' I said, remembering the magazine I'd seen at Helen's last year.

As I spoke, Angela parted her legs a little more. I glanced down and saw a hint of pink between her curls. Her clitoris had come into view. My index finger inched towards it.

'It doesn't have to be like that,' she said. 'Even if it is, it's a living. It can be a good living. You want to work in a factory all your life, spend all your time in an office?'

'Most people do.'

'You aren't most people.' She looked into my eyes.

189

'You remind me of myself at your age – although not so beautiful, of course! You're a great-looking girl, and a natural blonde. You've got the face, the figure. You could be very . . . ah . . . successful. I was, and I don't regret any of it. But we'll discuss this . . . ah . . . tomorrow. As I say, it's all up to you. If you want we can simply say goodbye, or if . . . if . . . ah . . . ah . . .'

She closed her eyes, and I gazed down as my finger encircled the tip of her clit. My other fingers joined it, stroking the moist lips of her twat. I bent my head over her left breast, sucking the delicious nipple between my lips; but this was only a postponement of what I should really have been sucking. I slid lower down the bed, my mouth gliding across Angela's warm skin, until my face was a few inches from her vagina. Her feminine odour was like some exotic perfume, the ultimate aphrodisiac.

I gazed in awe at the magic grotto which was her cunt, a wonderland of nature's architecture. This was the doorway which would lead Angela to total fulfillment, and I thrust my tongue towards her clitoris, guiding her towards the heights.

This was my first true taste of cunnilingus, and I discovered that giving was as fantastic as receiving.

Angela moaned with pleasure as my wet flesh caressed hers, and so did I.

I lay in bed for a long while the next morning, remembering every unbelievable thing that Angela and I had done together. We had both been insatiable and the night had lasted for hours. It was almost noon before I awoke, but she slept on by my side.

I wondered what I should do. It was all up to me, I knew. Angela and I owed each other nothing – although I would be forever indebted to her for the new dimensions of sexuality that she had revealed for my exploration.

Did I want to let her take explicit photographs of me? After what had happened between us, I would have allowed her to do whatever she wished. But did I want to become a nude model? Could I ever allow anyone else to picture me in such intimate poses?

She had offered to give me a lift away from town. I could live with her in the city if I wished. There would be no obligation. She had a spare room. I didn't have to pose for her. I didn't even have to fuck her.

And I didn't know what to do.

I gazed up into the mirror, studying myself and Angela, examining my own nude body and her perfect naked physique. With her so near, I couldn't think straight. As soon as she woke up again, we'd start making love once more. Although I desired yet another orgasm, I needed to get away for a while, and I managed to disentangle myself and climb out of bed.

I ran a comb through my hair and pulled on my T-shirt. My shorts were still damp from last night, and I couldn't find my knickers. But the T-shirt was long enough to be a mini-dress, so I opened the door of the honeymoon suite, went downstairs and crossed the road to the seafront.

For a long while I stood by the railings, gazing across the beach and out to sea. I'd no idea how much time passed while I was lost in my thoughts, but then I sensed Angela's presence. I turned, and she was crossing the road towards the promenade, a camera draped around her neck.

It was time to give her my answer.

I remembered staring up into the mirror above the bed, seeing Angela's sensuous body rapturously entwined with mine; and I remembered the mirror in my own bedroom, how I sometimes stretched in front of it, the way my T-shirt would ride up around my waist.

I stepped onto the lower rail and I leaned forward. As I did so, the back of my T-shirt slid up over my bare behind. I turned my head towards Angela – and she took my photograph.

It was the first of hundreds of photos which she was to take of me when I became a nude model; and those were only the first of thousands which other people would take.

But that's another story . . .

HONEY
will reveal even more in
CENTREFOLD
by
Angelique